M000233739

TROUBLE ON THE TRAIL

━━━━━━━━━━━━━ ✶ ━━━━━━━━━━━━━

Calhoun stuck the big Walker about two inches from the man's nose. "How many of you boys was there?" he asked quietly.

"Two," the man gasped. "Just me and Amos."

Calhoun nodded. "Where's your horses?"

"Got none." The man coughed and choked, the pain in his chest worsening.

Calhoun was surprised, and showed it. "Then why'd you shoot my animal?" he asked.

"Was aimin' for you," the man said.

"Explain it," Calhoun said with quiet determination.

"Wolves scared our horses off night before last. We been here since." His eyes drooped and he coughed.

Then the eyes cracked open and the chest rose feebly. "Then you come along. We figured to bushwhack you and take your horse." He tried to shrug, but the pain seared across him, stopping him in midmaneuver.

"Should've learned to shoot first," Calhoun commented wryly ...

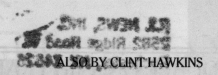

ALSO BY CLINT HAWKINS

SADDLE TRAMP
THE CAPTIVE

Published by
HarperPaperbacks

SADDLE TRAMP

GUNPOWDER TRAIL

---- ✱ ----

CLINT HAWKINS

HarperPaperbacks
A Division of HarperCollins Publishers

HarperPaperbacks   *A Division of* HarperCollins*Publishers*
10 East 53rd Street, New York, N.Y. 10022

Cover illustration by John Thompson

First printing: August 1992

Printed in the United States of America

HarperPaperbacks and colophon are trademarks of HarperCollins*Publishers*

❖ 10 9 8 7 6 5 4 3 2 1

CHAPTER

✳ 1 ✳

Wade Calhoun grabbed one of the Colt Walkers from the saddle holster and flung himself off the horse even before he heard the crack of a rifle. Having his hat ripped off by a bullet had been enough to set him in motion.

By the time he hit the ground, landing hard on his shoulder and rolling, the horse was down. The animal wasn't dead, but it was going fast. The echo of several more gunshots banged off the hillock behind Calhoun.

He quit rolling and came to a stop on his stomach. The Walker was cocked. Beyond the still kicking horse, he spotted puffs of gunsmoke from a brushy arroyo maybe seventy-five yards away.

The horse lay kicking in its death throes. The iron-shod hooves came dangerously close to Calhoun's head.

It was uncomfortable for Calhoun lying flat on his stomach, since the two Colt Dragoons he carried in cross-draw holsters dug into his belly that way. He considered putting another bullet in the horse, both to stop its kicking and to end the unfortunate animal's agony. He decided against it, though. He wanted whoever was out there to think he had been killed. If they thought so, they might come out from behind their cover. Then he would have them. If he shot the horse, they would know he was still alive.

So he bided his time, waiting, as the horse quivered, its kicks lessening. Finally the animal was still. Calhoun slid up behind the warm, still-quivering bulwark just as another shot rang out. A rifle ball slammed into the dead horseflesh. Calhoun rested the Walker up over the side of the animal and waited again.

He had no idea of how many men were in that arroyo, under the cover of the brush. Nor did he have a great desire to risk his neck to find out.

The spring sun beat hotly down on Calhoun's bare head. He glanced over his shoulder, looking longingly at his old slouch hat lying behind him. He cursed the misfortune.

Then he cursed the way that the horse had fallen. The animal was lying both on Calhoun's Henry rifle, and also on his canteen. It would have been nice to have the rifle, though the Walker most likely would be sufficient. He also had the two Dragoons, should the ambushers decide to charge his position.

The canteen, however, was another story. It would become absolutely necessary if this standoff lasted more than an hour or so. Already Calhoun could feel his tongue swelling up with the heat and thirst. He would have no relief from either. He sighed, unable to do anything but sit there wishing the horse had fallen the other way.

He was used to waiting, though, and he figured he could outlast these damn fools, whoever they were.

It wouldn't be easy, but he supposed he could afford to wait for a while.

On the other hand, he never did figure to live forever. Indeed, to some folks, it might seem that Wade Calhoun had actually been courting death these past few years. Ever since . . .

He pushed those thoughts away. Thinking about such things would do nothing but get him aggravated, or depressed, or both. He blanked his mind to all his troubles, and his hard, misfortune-filled past. His misfortune-filled present was enough to occupy his mind.

Calhoun shook his head ruefully. Damn, if it wasn't a horse getting him in trouble more often than not. He seemed to have a knack for picking horseflesh that had seen better days well before he came along.

When he was lucky enough to find a decent horse, the animal never seemed to last long. Usually, too, the horse brought with it a bellyful of trouble for Wade Calhoun.

"Damn it all anyhow," Calhoun muttered. The thoughts were firing him up. So was the heat from the sizzling, malevolent ball of a sun. He could not remember it being so hot this early in the year out here in northeastern Kansas Territory.

He pulled out his other big Walker—the one from the saddle holster that was more or less on top of the horse now. He checked the five loads he carried in it; and did the same with the first one. He hefted the two weapons, comfortable with their weight. Each was just under five pounds when loaded.

Calhoun nodded to himself. "Time's a-wastin', sure as hell," he muttered. He stood to his full five-foot-ten. Resigned determination was stamped across his pocked, ruggedly handsome face.

Then he charged the arroyo.

Gunfire cracked out from behind the brush and stunted trees. Bullets kicked up small clods of earth all around him, but none touched him.

Calhoun did use the gunfire, though, to make note of the enemies' position. From the puffs of gunsmoke, he figured there were two men in the thicket. There could be more, he realized; others who were not firing. He doubted that, though.

Less than twenty-five yards from the thicket, Calhoun flung himself down. He stopped, skidding and rolling, half on his stomach. He hoped they would think he had been shot. He didn't hold out much hope of that, since they had not seemed fooled before.

Calhoun waited only a heartbeat before firing. None of the ambushers had shown himself. So Calhoun simply fired twice from one pistol at where he estimated one of the men would be. He nodded in satisfaction when he heard a muffled grunt of pain. Not that he took enjoyment in killing, or even in inflicting pain. It was simply the satisfaction of having judged his target right, and a job well done.

A pistol ball ripped through his left sleeve, stinging his arm as it did.

"Son of a bitch," Calhoun snapped. He swung the Walker in his right hand in the other direction and pumped off the three remaining balls in it.

Calhoun heard a body falling in the thicket. He did not wait any longer, though. He shoved up and ran, heading for the cover of the brush.

He skidded to a stop behind a brushy, small willow and paused a moment to catch his breath.

He listened intently once his breathing has gotten back to normal. From his left—the direction of the second man at which he had fired—he heard nothing. From the right came some feeble moans, as well as the sounds of a man trying to crawl weakly through the clinging brush.

Calhoun stuck the empty Colt Walker in his belt and shifted the other to his right hand. With a nod, he slipped off through the trees and bushes, working toward his left. He moved silently, the low jingle of his spurs masked by the renewed chattering of birds and the wind soughing through the branches.

A few minutes later, he was kneeling beside the body of a nondescript man dressed in plain, soiled clothes. He had a hard look about him, even in death.

"Goddamn fool," Calhoun murmured.

Then he went through the man's pockets. He came up with eight dollars and seventy-five cents, all in coins. He dropped the money into his right front pants pocket, and stood.

As he turned to head in the other direction, he wondered where these men's horses were. He hoped they hadn't run off; he would want to use at least one for himself. He could use the other to bring the body or bodies to the nearest town.

Calhoun shrugged. That would wait until later, he

figured. He moved stealthily through the foliage again, making his way toward the first man he had shot.

It didn't take long to find him. The man had crawled some yards from where he had been shot, but he was in fairly bad shape. Calhoun strolled up behind him, Walker ready just in case. "Reckon y'all ought to take a rest, friend," Calhoun said quietly.

The man, still crawling, froze. Then his head sank down in defeat.

Calhoun bent over him and rolled the man over. He was as nondescript as the other, though perhaps a little younger. He was as shabbily dressed as the other and had a worn look about him. He also had a pained expression on his face. His breathing was labored, his chest working fitfully.

With a shake of his head at the stupidness of all this, Calhoun grabbed the man by the bloody shirt-front and lifted him a little. He did so with surprising ease, considering he was no giant. He dragged the man a little to the side and propped him in a half-sit against a tree trunk.

Calhoun stuck the big Walker about two inches from the man's nose. "How many of you boys was there?" he asked quietly.

"Two," the man gasped. "Just me and Amos."

Calhoun nodded. "Where's your horses?"

"Got none." The man coughed and choked, the pain in his chest worsening.

Calhoun was surprised, and showed it. "Then why'd you shoot my animal?" he asked.

"Was aimin' for you," the man said.

If he hadn't seen so much poor shooting in his life, Calhoun might have been inclined to disbelieve the man. But he had, so he didn't.

"Explain it," Calhoun said with quiet determination.

"Wolves scared our horses off night before last. We been here since." His eyes drooped and he coughed. To Calhoun it looked like he had expired.

Then the eyes cracked open and the chest rose feebly. "Then you come along. We figured to bushwhack you and take your horse." He tried to shrug, but the pain seared across him, stopping him in midmaneuver.

"Should've learned to shoot first," Calhoun commented wryly.

"Reckon you're right."

"Why didn't you just start walkin'?" Calhoun thought he knew, but he figured it was only right to ask.

The look in the dying man's eyes told him all he needed to know. These two over-the-hill, burned-out saddle bums figured it would be easier to just shoot down whoever was unlucky enough to come along instead of marching the three or four days to a town.

"What're you gonna do with me?" the man asked. He didn't sound scared. He was in too much agony for that.

Calhoun shrugged. "Ain't sure. You hadn't killed my horse, I might've been able to get you to a town somewhere."

"You could . . ."

"Could what?" Calhoun snapped. "You think I'm

gonna carry your stupid ass from here to wherever?" He snorted in disgust. After a moment he asked, "Where's your supplies?"

"Back there a little," the man said. He tried to lift his arm and point, but could only partly manage it.

"Don't go nowhere," Calhoun offered as he strolled away.

Within minutes he had found the small camp. He took a quick look around, seeing what the two men had in the way of food and all. There wasn't much, but he could manage to last for some days on it, even carrying some of it on his back.

He spun and headed back toward the wounded man, undecided as to what to do about him. He hoped an answer would present itself.

The man was still sitting against the tree, but he had managed to produce a pistol from somewhere. He had the small revolver cocked and pointed at the spot in the trees where Calhoun had left.

Calhoun, however, was not foolish enough to just walk in on the man cold like that. Not in the same spot. He stepped out from behind some brush a little to the man's right. His Walker was cocked and in hand.

"Best put that down," he warned quietly.

The man was so startled that he jerked, causing the pistol to fire.

"You could get hurt that way, boy," Calhoun offered.

"Bastard," the man muttered. He strained and struggled to cock the weapon again. At the same time, he half twisted so he could look at Calhoun.

"I'll kill you," he snapped, the hint of madness lurking in his eyes.

"Don't," Calhoun said simply.

The man did not stop. He finally managed to jerk the hammer back. With painful slowness, he began bringing the gun up.

Calhoun was not about to stand there and give this maniac a clear shot at him. He simply squeezed the trigger.

At this close range, the ball from the big Walker, pushed as it was by forty-five grains of powder, did awesome damage to the man's chest. The death throes sparked another shot from the man's pistol. The bullet tore off the man's own left big toe.

Calhoun shook his head again. He would never, he thought, cease to be amazed at the stupidity of some people.

He turned and made his way through the bushes and across the flat to his dead horse. Wolves, coyotes, and buzzards were already circling about the animal, though none had been brave enough to approach yet.

It took some work, but Calhoun finally managed to free his saddle. He would as soon leave one of his arms behind as that saddle. It and his weapons were his only valuable possessions.

Hiking the Spanish-style saddle with the tooled silver inlays over his shoulder, he headed back to the ambushers' camp.

CHAPTER

* 2 *

"**S**hit," Calhoun muttered as he squatted down amid the wreckage of his ill fortune.

He pulled out fixings and rolled a cigarette. After he lit it, he filled his tin mug with coffee from the pot the two ambushers had left on the small fire. Then he sat there, trying to decide just what he would do.

He could not stay here for long, that was certain. Scavengers would be after the two bodies—they were already working on his horse—before long. That was never a pleasant thing to listen to, but worse, it might encourage the wolves and coyotes to bother him.

There was not that much food in the packs. Besides, despite the stream, Calhoun figured there probably wasn't much game. The latter was due to one reason that he could see: Too many Indians in the area.

That, too, was a concern for Calhoun. Many of the tribes in northeast Kansas has been at least partially subjugated, but they were still known to cause trouble. Kickapoos, Kaws, Pawnees, even the Sioux, would come through here on raids.

Calhoun had seen the results of such raids far too

often. And more than once close up. He remembered one homestead here in the Kansas Territory in particular.

Such thoughts were with him always. It was a near constant fight, or so it seemed, to keep them from ruling his life. Time seemed to be allowing him some headway against the plaguing remembrances, but he knew they would never disappear.

Another byproduct of the harsh thoughts was that they had hardened Calhoun's heart against all Indians. He especially hated the Sioux, who had been the ones to raid that solitary homestead, and it had been his desire ever since to make the Sioux pay as often and as bloodily as possible.

Calhoun sighed and flicked the smoldering butt of his cigarette into the fire. The memories would get him nowhere. He had to decide what to do.

Hunger made him realize, though, that he didn't need to make a decision just yet. That could wait until after he ate.

He rooted through the packs until he came up with some salted beef, cornmeal, and beans. He prepared them as simply and quickly as he could and put them to cook. While he waited, he rolled another cigarette.

As he puffed, he checked over his other resources. He had had sixty-three dollars of his own. Combined with the almost nine dollars he had taken from the first body and the thirteen dollars and change taken from the second, he was better off than he had been in a long time.

Not that he was rich, of course, but he was better

off than he had been in a spell. He should have enough to buy himself a horse, at least, if he could get to a town.

He might even have enough left to get some supplies to tide him over for a while. Enough to get him to wherever it was he wanted to go next, when he figured that out.

Calhoun ate without much relish. It was odd, he had thought more than once, that he enjoyed being out on the trail since it had brought him much of the trouble he had seen in life. He quickly tired of trail food, though.

He didn't mind sleeping on the ground, and the snow and sun and heat and hardships of the trail. He hated the food, though, for the most part. Unless he could get buffalo. A steady diet of salted beef and bacon and beans and such paled quickly.

He didn't much like being in a town at all, except for the saloons and having decent food regularly.

He finished eating and wiped his greasy hands on his worn trousers. He looked down at his faded pants, ripped cotton shirt, and scuffed, trail-dusty boots. He almost smiled when he looked at his slouch hat lying on the ground next to his right foot. He had retrieved that when he had gotten his saddle earlier. The hat was in terrible shape. It had been sweat-stained, pocked with holes and generally foul looking. Now it sported two new bullet holes—one in, one out.

Maybe he would get some new clothes whenever he got to town. Then he decided that these were serviceable enough for a while yet. Better he should save his money for something more vital, or entertaining.

Calhoun cleaned his two Walkers, oiling them down carefully with the bottle of sperm oil he always carried with him. While he worked, he sipped coffee from his tin cup.

After slipping the Walkers into the saddle holsters, Calhoun checked over his other weapons. The rifle had taken a beating when the horse went down atop it. It seemed fine, though. Calhoun also checked his Colt Dragoons, since they had been shoved into the dirt more than once while he had been rolling around on the ground. They, too, were fine.

Finished, Calhoun rolled a cigarette. He puffed it and sipped from a pint bottle of whiskey he had found among the dead men's effects. His choices were limited as to what to do. There were only a handful of towns within a week's walk of here; none of them of any size. They would not have much of a selection of horses or supplies.

No, he decided, it would have to be St. Joe. He figured it would take a little more than a week to reach the place, but it should be worth it. St. Joseph, Missouri, was a populous town, and a growing center as a jumping-off place for the Oregon Trail. Calhoun knew that he would have a wide selection of horses there, as well as several stores plentifully stocked with goods.

In addition, there was the likelihood that he would be able to sign on as a guide for one of the wagon trains—should he decide he needed a job.

The decision had been easy, despite his earlier misgivings. He had known all along, though, that it would be. It was just his way to nibble at the problem for a spell before setting it aside. Once he did that, the answer always came nice and simply.

Calhoun stood and stretched, and looked up at the sky. The sun was still high, but it was at least two hours past noon. He thought of leaving here now. He could make ten miles or more, walking steadily, if he left now.

He decided against it, though. He was tired, and this camping spot looked comfortable. Morning would be early enough, he decided.

He spent the next hour or so, culling out what supplies he thought absolutely necessary to have with him. There was too much, so he made a second pass through the items. He finally ended with enough to fill one gunnysack. If he was sparing in his use of the supplies, they should last him to St. Joseph.

He sat, leaning back against his saddle, half dozing. The startled burst of small birds fleeing jolted him awake some time later. He stayed in the same position he had been in, though. His only real movement was to edge his right hand across his midsection and ease out a Dragoon.

His ears picked out the quickly muffled snort of a horse. He stood in one fluid motion and in three steps was behind a small cottonwood. He waited patiently. After a few minutes, Calhoun sensed that whoever was out there was standing just on the other side of the clearing, checking the place out.

Soon after, a painted Kickapoo warrior eased into the small campsite clearing. He went straight to the fire and knelt, checking out the fire, the coffeepot, Calhoun's mug, the debris of life lying there. He turned his head and spoke briefly in his own language.

A few minutes later, Calhoun heard another Indian shout from the direction of one of the bodies. Then a third voice from where Calhoun had killed the second man. Within moments, three Kickapoos were gathering around the fire, laughing at the foolishness of white men killing each other.

Calhoun still waited behind the tree, wanting to see if there were any other warriors. There didn't seem to be, and when the three started looking his handsome saddle over, he stepped out from his cover. The cocked Dragoon was in his hand.

"Afternoon, boys," he said flatly.

The three Indians whirled, startled. One carried an old muzzle-loading trade rifle with a feather tied around the barrel near the muzzle. He started to bring the weapon up.

Calhoun waggled the Colt, and shook his head. The Indian lowered the rifle again.

"Move away from the saddle."

The warriors edgily did as they were told.

"Sit," Calhoun said. His heart was cold as stone toward Indians, but he had had enough killing for one day—unless more became necessary.

The Indians sat warily. Still keeping an eye on them, Calhoun shuffled to where he had tossed the things he would not need to take with him. He bent, never taking his eyes off the Indians, and picked up three cups and tossed them to the Indians.

"Coffee's free," he said.

The three nodded solemnly and poured coffee for themselves. They talked quietly among themselves a moment, and Calhoun figured they were plotting his demise.

He sat, his back against the saddle. "Any of you boys speak English?" he asked.

Three sets of dark eyes looked blankly back at him. Calhoun figured at least one of them could speak some English, and maybe all of them. Still, it was the Indian way, Calhoun figured, to be stubborn.

Calhoun shrugged. "Don't put me out none," he allowed. "I wasn't plannin' to chat with you damn fools anyway."

He paused, and wiggled the Dragoon a moment. "'Course, I could just shoot your asses flat dead here and now, savin' me some grief later." His face was hard, and a sneer curled his lip.

"I speak your tongue," one offered quietly. His words were heavily accented and his speech guttural.

"What do you want here?"

"We heard gunfire."

Calhoun nodded. It was plausible enough. But he had killed those men a couple of hours ago. He hated to think these three had been lurking about all that time. He decided they had not, since they would have known he was here. Their surprise when he had appeared had been genuine. Of that he was sure.

He faced a dilemma now. These three would have

at least one horse each. They might even have some extras. He thought he could buy one, maybe even two, from them if they had extra. He was also cold-hearted enough that he would be more than happy to just take one from them at gunpoint, if they had no extras.

To do that, though, he would have to walk three warriors through a brushy thicket to get to their horses. Or send one of them to get the horses while he held the other two hostage. Either would likely be fatal, the latter the more so.

"Where's your horses?"

The Indian who spoke before shrugged. "Run away," he said. He put a pained expression on his face, like he was disgusted with himself for having let it happen.

"Bullshit," Calhoun said quietly.

The Indian glared at him. He suddenly realized he was not dealing with some stupid settler or one of the even more foolish missionaries who pestered his village too often.

"Back there." The warrior jerked his head toward the brush to Calhoun's right.

"What's your name?"

"Walkin' Thunder."

"You got any extra horses, Walkin' Thunder?"

"Maybe," Walking Thunder said shrewdly.

"I'll buy one or two of 'em from you."

"With what?"

Calhoun shrugged. "Anything in the camp 'cept this here saddle, my personal belongin's, and that gunnysack over there." He pointed with the Dragoon.

Walking Thunder thought for a few moments. Then he nodded. "It is good," he offered. He and his two companions started to stand.

They froze, though, when Calhoun said quietly, "Not so fast, boys." When the Indians had resettled their behinds on the ground, Calhoun said, "I reckon we ought to go take a look at them horses before you start loadin' your booty."

"Light Weasel'll bring them," Walking Thunder said.

One of the other warriors nodded.

"No," Calhoun said flatly. "We'll go together." He stood. With the pistol, he indicated that the Indians should follow suit.

When they had done so, Calhoun said, "You boys found them bodies out there. I killed both of 'em. I'll not regret doin' the same to you should you pull any foolishness on our walk." He glared for a moment, making sure they knew he was speaking the truth.

"Now move," Calhoun said harshly.

The three spun and headed into the brush. Calhoun followed closely behind. He was tense, wary. He knew there was no other real choice, though. He had to take the chance.

Suddenly the three Kickapoos just disappeared. One moment they were marching ahead of Calhoun in the break in the foliage that formed something of a path; the next, they were gone. The only sign of their going was a few branches swaying from their passage.

Calhoun cursed silently. In the blink of an eye, he had slid behind a tree and fired once in the direction he thought Light Weasel had gone. A muffled grunt popped out from the brush.

A few moments later, Calhoun heard horses galloping away.

"Shit," he muttered. But he stayed where he was. It could be a trick.

CHAPTER

* 3 *

Calhoun waited for about half an hour. If the Kickapoos had really left, he didn't want to stay there too long and give them a chance to return. If they hadn't left, he might as well face them and get it over with.

He moved silently through the thicket, making his way toward where Light Weasel had vanished. He found the Indian's body before too long. He knew it had been a lucky shot that had killed the Kickapoo, but he was not about to worry about that now.

The death did present another problem, though. He figured that the Kickapoos, like most other of the Indians that roamed the Plains, would not be happy at leaving the body of a friend behind. He was certain they would be back sooner or later. He only hoped it was later.

Calhoun spun and headed back to his camp. Though he was moving quickly, he was also moving cautiously. One could never be sure that the Kickapoos hadn't just ridden a quarter mile away, curled around and were waiting for him.

He circled the campsite through the foliage, but found no one. He finally entered it. He scooped up his cup, dumped the contents on the ground, and shoved the cup into one of his saddlebags. He grabbed the saddle—with bedroll and saddlebags attached—in one hand. Hoisting it, he grabbed the gunnysack in the other hand.

Then he moved out, leaving the fire burning.

He finally came out on the south side of the thicket. Stopping just before that, he surveyed the rolling, grassy plains ahead of him. He saw nothing. It didn't mean nothing was there, he knew; but if there was something out there, it was staying hidden.

He moved onto the grassy sward, walking with long, certain strides. Once he had made up his mind to act, little would sway him.

It was not long before darkness overtook him. Calhoun was fortunate enough, though, to find another small copse that would offer shelter and some protection.

He made a small fire quickly, heated coffee, and cooked a meal. As soon as the coffee was hot and the food cooked, he kicked dirt over the fire, extinguishing it. It was not full dark yet, but that would not be long in coming. He did not want even a small fire giving him away.

Full, he finally spread out his bedroll. From the small of his back, he pulled his reserve pistol and tossed it aside, close to hand. It was an old Colt Walker. He had cut the barrel down to two inches. At close range, it was a devastating weapon, especially when it was a surprise to an enemy.

Calhoun stretched out on his blanket and canvas bedroll on his back. It had been a long day, and he was tired. Pulling his hat over his eyes, he was asleep almost instantly.

He felt refreshed in the morning. After taking care of personal business, he had a quick look around. Seeing nothing out of the ordinary, he built another small fire and made his breakfast.

The meal was small and rapidly eaten, and with less than overwhelming enthusiasm. It took Calhoun only minutes to gather up his few loose belongings, roll up his bedroll, and tie it behind the saddle. Once more he hefted the heavy saddle and the gunnysack and marched off.

The day was long, hot, tiring and filled Calhoun with boredom. He didn't mind the latter so much, considering it meant that the Kickapoos had not found him. Nor had any other hostile Indians. He was glad for that.

He was not so glad for that night's accommodations. He walked as long as he dared, but he never found any shelter or water. He had a cold meal of buffalo jerky, dry biscuits and water from his canteen. He was sick of jerky, too, but he was happy he had some along on him. Otherwise, he would have gone hungry.

Soon after finishing the disagreeable meal, Calhoun spread out his bedroll and turned in.

The next day contained more of the same. The next night, too, though he managed to stop early enough that there was some daylight left. In the fading light, he was able to gather enough buffalo chips to create a small fire. The flames burned hot but not for long. Still, they lasted long enough for him to get a small pot of coffee made and some beans and salted beef cooked.

In a somewhat better frame of mind, he turned in. Having hot coffee and sizzling bacon for breakfast improved his spirits a little more. Even his aching feet and sore shoulders could not dampen his joy much.

Also helping to hearten him was the fact that he still had not seen the Kickapoos. He was hoping that they might have been discouraged and gone home. Either that or were having trouble picking up his trail. He didn't much care which. He figured that if he could keep to the rate he was traveling, he would be in St. Joseph in four days; possibly even three.

He was marching along at a pretty good clip. He felt as glad as he ever had in the past few years, which wasn't very, but it was better than the dourness he usually carried with him. He was moving at such a good pace and watching out for hostile Indians that he was not paying much attention to where his feet were going. He stepped in a chuckhole.

Without the heavy saddle and the gunnysack, he might have been able to catch himself more easily. With those two items, though, he listed to his right, feeling the ankle twist under him.

Calhoun dropped the saddle as he fell, reaching out his arm to catch himself. He felt a short, sharp pain in his right ankle.

"Damn it all to hell and back," he growled, as he landed heavily. He pushed up until he was sitting. Pulling off his right boot, he probed the ankle with his fingers. He winced once or twice, but then realized it wasn't all that bad. It would hamper his speed, though, which would add to the time it would take to reach St. Joseph.

He took a deep breath to settle his anger. His good feelings had vanished already. Then he pulled on his boot. He stood, testing the ankle gingerly. It would hold him.

Calhoun grabbed his saddle and sack and limped off, muttering curses. He grew more and more irritable as the day wore on. The pain in his ankle increased a bit, and he slowed his pace again to accommodate it. The day's heat was fierce, and the gusty wind brought dust that slapped at his face. He was dirty, hungry, and more than a little irritable.

"All I need now is for those damned Kickapoos to show up again," he said aloud. There was no one to hear him, which was fine with him.

They eventually did find him.

Late in the afternoon, he heard a soft rumble. He stopped and cocked his head. It was, he figured, either buffalo or horses running. The sound grew louder but not in depth. That meant, Calhoun realized, that there were not many of the animals, whatever they were.

Calhoun stood there, and turned in a slow, deliberate circle, seeking out the source of the noise. At last he spotted a small cloud of dust to the northwest. It was moving fast. Suddenly two Kickapoos popped up over the apex of a ridge. They were riding hell-for-leather toward Calhoun.

There was no place for Calhoun to run. He shrugged and dropped his saddle and supplies. It was a relief to have them not dragging on his shoulders.

He pulled out his rifle, made sure the cap was in place, and knelt.

As he brought the rifle up to his shoulder, the warriors disappeared below the horizon, hidden by another swell. They eventually came out again, up onto the crest of a hillock. When they did, Calhoun was ready.

He had never taken the rifle down off his shoulder. He also had estimated where they would show up the next time. He set his sights accordingly. When the warriors hove into view once again, he hurriedly aimed and squeezed off a shot.

One of the warriors tumbled from his saddle. At almost three hundred yards, Calhoun could not be sure if it was Walking Thunder or the Indian whose name he did not know. He did not care much, either.

As the second slipped below the next rise, Calhoun reloaded his rifle with practiced ease and speed. He knelt there, waiting, rifle up again.

Calhoun had miscalculated this time, though. Or else the Kickapoo had become wiser after his companion had been shot down. The warrior came into view several score yards to the south of where Calhoun had been expecting. Calhoun caught the movement in the corner of his eye and swung that way. He fired.

The bullet kicked up a puff of dust as the warrior vanished again.

"Damn fool," Calhoun muttered at himself.

The Kickapoo materialized again, only fifty yards away this time. Calhoun noted that it was Walking Thunder. He had reloaded his rifle and took aim. He fired.

"Shit," he said aloud.

Walking Thunder seemed to have anticipated his shot and jerked his pony's head to the right at the last minute. It might have been coincidental, but whichever, Calhoun cursed at having missed his shot. He was usually dead on with either rifle or pistol, seeming to have a second sense with a gun in hand. It always irritated him when he missed, especially at a target so close.

He shrugged. Walking Thunder was bearing down on him with a rush, and he had no time to worry about having missed.

Calhoun dropped the rifle to the ground next to him, and snatched one of the Walkers from a saddle holster. Still kneeling, he rested his right elbow on his right knee and aimed. Then he patiently squeezed off four rounds.

The Kickapoo's howling war cry changed to cries of pain as all the slugs from the cap-and-ball revolver hit him. One broke his upper right arm, another his left shin; the third punched a hole in his face, just under the left eye; the fourth hit the chest.

Walking Thunder fell and bounced several times before stopping. He lay there as the dust settled.

His pony had kept running. Calhoun dropped his Walker, hobbled two steps, and then dived, arms straining to catch the rope rein tied to the horse's lower jaw.

He missed and landed heavily, grunting with the impact. Then he swore, steadily and with verve. He cursed his continuing string of misfortune, and all

Indians. He swore at horses in general, and the fleeing Kickapoo pony in particular.

Once he had gotten that out of his system, he picked up the Walker again and headed toward Walking Thunder. The Kickapoo was dead, covered with blood.

Calhoun limped on, heading toward the other Kickapoo. That warrior also was dead. Buzzards had already settled on him and been pecking away for a few minutes. Calhoun stood there, looking down. He felt neither joy nor remorse. These Kickapoos had chosen their course and gone the limit. Calhoun had done the only thing he could.

He considered taking the time to bury the two Indians. The notion died aborning. He decided that neither deserved it. He did not want to spend the time, either, and he had no shovel. With a shrug, he turned and walked back to his saddle.

After cleaning and reloading his rifle and the Walker, he took the time for a cigarette. He sat there on his fancy saddle, forcing himself to keep his mind blank.

Finally he crushed the cigarette butt underfoot. With a sigh of annoyance, Calhoun grabbed his things and hobbled eastward.

He bagged a deer late in the afternoon, and found a decent campsite for the night. There was a stream moving sluggishly though clearly nearby, and there was plenty of wood.

With mildly rejuvenated spirits, Calhoun built a fire, put coffee on, hacked out a venison steak, and tossed the meat into a fry pan. He sat back to wait for his supper. To pass the time, he finished off the last bit of whiskey in the pint bottle he had taken from the two men he had killed.

He tossed the bottle into the bushes and dug into his half-raw venison steak. The succulent meat was washed down with harsh, bitter coffee.

Calhoun wondered whether he should move on. It was possible that other Kickapoos were following Walking Thunder. Then he shrugged and smiled viciously into the darkness. "Let 'em come," he murmured as he spread out his bedroll.

He spent the next day and the next night there. He had everything he could need here, and he figured to give his ankle a little time to heal. Also, he held out just a ray of hope that one of the Kickapoo ponies might wander into the thicket.

That did not happen, and he finally walked on. His ankle was considerably better, but he kept his pace slower than when he had started.

Four days later, he spotted St. Joseph across the muddy Missouri River. He paid out more than he thought he should for a ferry ride across, and then shuffled into the bustling town.

The first thing he did was get a room at a hotel. He dropped his things off and then set out for the first restaurant he could find. After eating his fill of ham and chicken and potatoes and apple pie, he drifted to a brothel.

An hour later, feeling quite human again, he wandered through the swinging bat-wing doors of the Last Look, a low dive of a saloon. He had taken care of all his appetites but one.

CHAPTER

4

Calhoun sat in the Last Look, quietly but with determination drinking his life away.

He was making pretty good progress at it when a burly, harried-looking man moved up to the table. "Mind if'n I set a spell?" the man asked.

"Suit yourself," Calhoun said coldly. He did not want company, but he was too full of tarantula juice to want to argue over a chair either.

"You're drunk," the man said. It did not sound like an accusation, merely a statement of fact.

"I am," Calhoun acknowledged. His manner did not lighten any.

"My name's Barrett Coldhammer," the man said.

Calhoun shrugged. He didn't rightly give a damn. All he wanted was to be left alone with his whiskey and his bad memories.

Coldhammer grimaced but then said, "You've got a hell of a reputation for bringin' wagon trains through safely, Mister Calhoun." It was obvious he was not pleased at Calhoun's sodden condition.

"I do," Calhoun slurred, keeping blurry but wary eyes on Coldhammer.

Calhoun had done plenty of scouting for wagon trains heading for California and Oregon, and even down south, along the Santa Fe Trail. He had stayed away from such things of late, though, finding them too tedious.

Still, his interest was piqued a little. The thought of guiding another wagon train did not excite him, but it was a way to bring in some much-needed cash.

"I got a wagon train set to jump off tomorrow at first light, heading for Oregon," Coldhammer said. "You want to guide it?"

"How many?" Calhoun said, words falling over each other in a sloshing jumble.

"Fourteen wagons, plus extra horses and mules. There's twenty-one men and—"

"Dollars, damnit," Calhoun rasped. "How many goddamn dollars are you payin'?"

"Two hundred," Coldhammer said quietly. He cast a sternly reproving look on Calhoun.

Calhoun didn't really want the job. He didn't want to deal with the plodding oxen. Or hear the squawling children who, if he let them, would remind him of his little Lottie. He did not want to put up with the half-dead men who would start the trip with wild dreams of glory reflected in their eyes but who would be beaten and broken halfway along.

Calhoun might be drunker than a lord, but he still had the common sense God had given him. Even with the money he had taken from the two ambushers, he didn't have much. It would be barely enough to get a horse and something of a grubstake. Taking a job leading a wagon train, though, could set him up for a spell.

It was either take this job offer, or eventually be forced to go off and rob a stage or something similar. Such a thing would not be a first for him, though it was always a last resort.

"I get half tomorrow. Other half when we get there." Calhoun looked at Coldhammer with a question in his eyes.

"Acceptable."

"And a horse."

"Agreed."

"Grub and any supplies I need."

"That, too." Coldhammer sounded weary.

"Meet you at the grove just north of town. Near the ferry." He tilted up his glass and drained the rotgut.

Coldhammer stood. "I expect you to be sober on this trip, Mister Calhoun," he said severely, casting a sharp look at Calhoun. "We don't need a guide who can't shoot straight because he is incapacitated by strong drink. Nor one who can't keep his wits about him. Strong drink has been the downfall of many men. And I daresay that a goodly number of them were better men than you."

"You don't think I can hold up my end?" Calhoun demanded in icy tones.

"Not in your condition, sir," Coldhammer said stiffly. He was already regretting his decision to hire Calhoun.

Suddenly one of the Colt Dragoons appeared in Calhoun's hand. The hand was steady as a rock. Coldhammer blanched as the big black hole of the muzzle pointed steadily at his forehead.

With his left hand, Calhoun snatched a single silver dollar from the table in front of him and flipped it upward. The piece of metal twirled into the air. The Dragoon swung around, tracking it. Three shots rang out in rapid succession. Silence descended over the saloon as hard-eyed men dove for cover and sought out the source of the gunfire.

The coin pinged softly and jerked three times as bullets winged it, making it dance in the air. It fell with a quietly ringing clink on the bar.

Calhoun had never questioned the fact that liquor seemed to have no effect on his shooting eye. Indeed, he hardly ever thought about it. He simply accepted it for something that he was blessed—or maybe cursed—with and let it go at that. It had, however, saved his hide on more than one occasion.

Calhoun swung around again so that the cocked Colt Dragoon was pointed at Coldhammer once more.

"Any more doubts?" he asked in a voice cold as a Sierra Nevada winter.

"No," Coldhammer squeaked.

The saloon was coming back to life again. The noise level grew and swelled. The cloud of acrid blue gunsmoke surrounding Calhoun began to dissipate.

"Tomorrow," Calhoun growled. "The grove. North of town."

Coldhammer slunk away, regretting having hired Wade Calhoun and cursing himself for the cowardice he thought he had showed. He also was relieved to be out of Calhoun's presence.

Calhoun poured another drink, emptying the bottle. He finished the liquor. For a moment he considered ordering another. He knew that would be stupid, though, considering he had just been hired on to lead a wagon train that was moving out at dawn.

He stood unsteadily and pocketed his cash. Then he shoved the Dragoon into the holster and strolled out.

He was hungover but mobile in the morning, after several large cups of black coffee and a hot breakfast. When he finished, he staggered out into the still-dark, fresh morning and moseyed to the nearest livery stable.

There he paid the livery man three dollars. He walked back to the hotel to get his things while the livery man harnessed a cart.

Calhoun was waiting outside the hotel when the driver came by. Calhoun threw his saddle and gunnysack of supplies into the back and gingerly climbed up onto the seat next to the driver.

The young man was maybe seventeen, and fresh faced despite the hour. Calhoun disliked him immediately. His dislike grew as the young man kept trying to start a conversation.

Finally Calhoun turned bloodshot eyes on the young man. The driver, of course, could not see the depths of Calhoun's hangover, which was unfortunate. Even he would have known enough to shut up if he could see those red-tinged holes in Calhoun's rugged, pocked face.

He couldn't though. It took a growled, "Shut your

yap, boy, and drive," from Calhoun before the young man caught on that this hard, high-smelling passenger did not want conversation. He shut up and drove, feeling a cold trickle run up his spine.

The driver was glad to be shed of Calhoun when he dropped him off at the grove of cottonwoods and willows. Calhoun grabbed his gear and marched into the travelers' camp.

Coldhammer moved out to greet him, shaking his hand. "Didn't think you was gonna show," Coldhammer said. He had tried to sound apologetic, but he was too unsure of himself right now for that.

"Well, I'm here." Calhoun was even more surly than usual.

Coldhammer nodded, and coughed in his confusion. He was not quite sure what to think—or do—about a man like Wade Calhoun.

"Where's my cash?" Calhoun asked. He dropped his saddle and sack and held out his hand. He said nothing as he accepted the hundred dollars in gold coins that Coldhammer gave him.

"My horse?" Calhoun asked.

"Don't you want to meet the folks first?" Coldhammer asked. His surprise showed on his beefy face.

"No." The single, cold word confused Coldhammer all the more.

The wagon master finally shrugged. "All right," he said. "Stow your gear over there." He pointed to his own wagon. "It'll be safe."

Calhoun nodded and moved his things, dropping them next to the rear off-wheel. He caught a flicker in his eye. In the burgeoning of the dawn, he spotted the pale, dim outline of a pretty girl's face. She was peering surreptitiously at him from the cover of the wagon.

He walked with Coldhammer to the horse herd. It wasn't a large herd, but there seemed to be some choice animals in the lot.

"Take your pick," Coldhammer said, waving his right hand magnanimously.

Calhoun took his time wandering through the herd, looking the animals over. Though he had poor luck with horses in the long run, there were times he could pick out a good one. The animal wouldn't last, he knew, but he wanted one he could rely on for as long as he could manage.

He finally choose a chesty, walleyed skewbald. The horse was rather funny looking, but it seemed to have stamina. The animal also appeared to be strong enough to carry Calhoun's heavy saddle for long periods without complaint.

Calhoun brought the horse to Coldhammer's wagon and tied the animal to the wheel near the saddle. He hated to do it; indeed, he wanted to get on the trail now that daylight was here, but he knew he was going to have to meet the others sooner or later.

He reluctantly let Coldhammer introduce him around. Calhoun was not the most sociable man under the best of circumstances. With his pounding head and roiling guts, he was downright surly.

As he finally got around to saddling the skewbald horse, he figured that had gotten him off on the wrong foot with most of the people in the wagon train. He really didn't give a damn, though. He had been hired to do a job, not run a church social or make friends. He wouldn't want most of these people as friends anyway.

As soon as the horse was ready, Calhoun pulled himself into the saddle. "Let's move," he bellowed. His voice made his head pound all the more.

"Damn," he muttered, shutting his eyes a moment. He hoped the roaring in his head and the dancing spots before his eyes would go away. He opened his eyes again, and was relieved to be able to see almost normally. Just a bit of a blur clouded his vision.

He swung the horse around and headed toward the river.

Coldhammer had made arrangements earlier to ferry the wagon train and all its accoutrements across the Missouri. It was done more swiftly than most of the people on the wagon train had figured. Calhoun, however, chafed at the agonizing slowness with which it proceeded.

Finally, though, everyone and everything was on the west bank of the river and the wagon train was moving.

Calhoun trotted out to where he would be far enough ahead of the lead wagons to not have to eat any dust. He was not so far away, though, that he had to worry too much about an Indian attack. He didn't really suspect anything like that this close to the settlements, but one could never be sure. He had not gotten as far as he had in life by lacking caution.

By the time he settled the skewbald into an easy

walk, he had already forgotten most of the names he had heard of the travelers. There were a few of the folks he would remember for whatever reason—six hard-looking men and two attractive young women, in particular. Most of the people were inconsequential to him and so he put them out of his mind right away.

He was some glad to be out ahead of the plodding wagons and their dull occupants. Calhoun had never cottoned to such people and usually kept his distance from them.

On the other hand, being out here alone like this gave him time to think. And that was not something he wanted to do. Whenever he did, his thought turned to a homestead here in Kansas Territory . . . a young woman named Lizbeth . . . an infant girl named Lottie.

"Damn," he hissed as he forced his mind away from these thoughts. He turned his thoughts instead to the land around him.

Most people, he knew, figured that this was the easiest part of his job, being just outside of St. Joseph. It wasn't, though. It was a pleasant enough looking area, though rather flat and treeless for Calhoun's taste. Calhoun preferred the wooded, well-watered hollows of his Kentucky childhood, even though he had left there years ago.

Farms were scattered haphazardly about here. It was June and the land was in bloom. Grasses grew tall and green, rustling in the constant wind. Wildflowers sprouted in colorful profusion. Crops were beginning to rise.

Despite the pleasantness of the land around here, being this close to civilization made Calhoun's job difficult. Game was hard to come by, water often was fouled, and wood for the cookfires usually was scarce.

In addition, he had to guide the wagons around farms, lest they incur the wrath of the farmers. Finding good campsites was hard, too, what with all the wagon trains passing this way. With the rains of late, the trail was rutted, making the ride—or walk—torture.

Several times, Calhoun made use of the slight humps of ridges that popped up frequently. He stopped and sat on his horse, watching the slow progress of the wagons. He drank more water than he was used to, trying to calm the fires of hangover that burned in his belly. It did little good.

CHAPTER
* 5 *

By the time the sun had passed its zenith, Calhoun began ranging even farther out, swinging in a lazy arc north to south ahead of the wagon train. It was time to start looking for a place to spend the night.

At times like these, Calhoun was glad he had experience along this trail. He knew the water holes and streams. He knew where there were groves of trees.

He was wild enough to push his people longer than most guides would, so they would not be stuck in campsites that had been overused by earlier travelers. Most times, those who hired him were not aware of that. He knew that more of them than not would not be pleased at the long hours he forced them into. Calhoun, however, was unconcerned with that thought.

By midafternoon he had passed two spots that had been used heavily, and fairly recently. He grinned sourly, knowing that by the time his charges passed these spots they would be grumbling.

An hour later he passed another likely campsite. This one had been used less harshly than the others, but the water still was fouled and dry wood was scarce. Calhoun pressed on.

Just before dark, Calhoun found a spot he thought would do. He stopped, dismounted, and loosened his saddle to let the horse breathe. He walked around, assuring himself that the trickle of a stream would provide sufficient water for the train's needs and that there was enough dry wood.

Satisfied, he tightened the saddle cinch and loped back toward the wagons.

Barrett Coldhammer was almost frantic. Darkness was nearly full on them and there had been no sign that Calhoun was anywhere in the vicinity. Some of the emigrants had begun to think—out loud —that Calhoun had taken his hundred dollars and had ridden back to St. Joseph.

Coldhammer was beginning to believe them when Calhoun came into view.

"Why ain't we stopped yet, Calhoun?" Coldhammer demanded. "It's damn near dark."

"No likely place."

"Hell, we've passed by several spots that've been used by other wagon trains. If it was good enough for those others, it should've been good enough for us."

"There was no wood, no water," Calhoun said simply.

"But . . ."

Calhoun shrugged. "We can argue till dawn, if you want. Or you can move these folks a little faster. I've staked out a spot about two miles on."

Calhoun clamped his mouth shut. He had just made one hell of a speech for him. He needed to give his voice a rest.

He supposed he could stand here and explain things to Coldhammer—or to the whole wagon train, if necessary—to ease the wagon master's mind. He knew, though, that such a thing would do none of them any good and only waste time.

Calhoun turned his horse and slowly rode off.

Coldhammer had a choice: Stop where he was, or follow Calhoun. He waved his arm and moved ahead. He was angry at Calhoun, and he knew he would have a near mutiny on his hands if Calhoun continued to behave like he had this first day. Coldhammer suspected, though, that there was little likelihood of Calhoun changing his ways.

The wagon master also figured there was little he could do about it all now. He would have to wait till the people started getting out of hand. Then he would deal with it in a way he thought best.

Coldhammer turned back and stopped by each wagon. He encouraged the people to move a little faster. In the gathering dusk, Calhoun was barely visible out ahead. Coldhammer did not want to have to miss a good campsite because the people were traveling too slowly.

The wagon master had to admit that the campsite seemed to be a good one after they had pulled into the small grove of cottonwoods. It was night now, but an almost full moon spread enough light that they could see by.

The people did grumble, not very loudly but consistently. They growled about the long day on the trail. They snarled about having to make their camp in the dark. They whined about having to tend to the animals without real light. They protested having to gather wood under the pale glimmer of the moon. They fretted at being forced to sup so late. They complained that their oxen, mules, and horses —and themselves—would not get enough rest.

Calhoun ignored the grumbling with practiced aplomb. He was used to such things, and had a tough enough hide that it did not bother him. People were people, and they would grumble and complain about something. This gave them something to focus their criticisms on.

As long as no one challenged him directly on any of it, he didn't mind. If someone wanted to throw it in his face, though, well that would be an entirely different matter. They would be taking their lives in their own hands in such a case.

Calhoun led his horse away from the rough circle of wagons. As always, he wanted to be alone.

He was as hungry as a bear, and the residual effect of last night's indulgence still lingered in his system.

He felt better, though, in having brought these people through their first day on the trail. They might not know it, but that was something of an accomplishment. Not much of one, but something.

Calhoun unsaddled his horse away from the others a little and set his fancy saddle down at the base of a cottonwood.

He took his time brushing the animal down. Since he had just gotten the steed that morning, he had not formed an attachment to it. He seldom did such a thing anyway, not with his luck with horses. He simply looked at the horse as he did his pistols— something that was necessary and if cared for would be of use to him. As he cared carefully for his guns, he cared carefully for whatever mount he had at the time.

When he had finished tending the animal, he hobbled it and turned it out to graze. Then he headed toward Coldhammer's fire, where he figured he would take his meals. It was usual for the guide—or at least him when he was a guide—to sup at the captain's fire.

He sat, silently thankful that the hangover had diminished considerably, though it had not disappeared.

He ate in sullen silence, letting the Coldhammers know he did not want to be bothered.

At first, Coldhammer's wife, Martha, tried to be cheerful, but Calhoun was not having any of it. The woman soon learned to leave him be. She clamped a sour look on her pudgy face and waited on her husband.

Calhoun was, however, more than a little interested in Coldhammer's daughter, Polly.

Where Martha Coldhammer was short and round with matronly plumpness, her daughter was fairly tall and slim, with a young woman's desirable litheness.

Calhoun took some small amount of hidden pleasure in watching Polly Coldhammer. Especially in seeing that she seemed quite interested.

Since this was their first night out on the trail, he decided it was not the time nor the place for him to approach her.

After eating, Calhoun dropped his plate and cup in the dirt. He shoved to his feet and stalked away. He spread his bedroll out away from the others, under the branches of the cottonwood where he had stored his saddle. After taking care of his personal needs, he turned in. He was asleep almost by the time he was stretched out.

Calhoun ate a silent breakfast at the Coldhammers' fire the next morning. Then he rode out. He had spoken to no one. The only sign of humanity he had displayed was the occasional soft smile he cast at Polly Coldhammer.

The girl had blushed each time, but the second time he had done it, she returned it shyly.

Calhoun set a good, steady pace and kept it up throughout the day. Once again he kept the travelers going long past when they thought they should stop.

Each day for the next week it was the same for the wagon train—an early start; a hard, just-short-of-punishing pace; and a late halt under the blanket of stars.

The complaining by the travelers seemed to grow in strength, volume, and intensity with each day they were out. By the end of their first week on the trail, a goodly number of the emigrants were on the verge of mutiny.

The main trouble had come on the first Sunday out. The objections at even the thought of traveling on the Sabbath reached such a crescendo that Calhoun disgustedly shook his head.

Coldhammer used all his persuasion to defuse the situation. As captain, he had complete authority over the group, though he was still reluctant to use it.

He finally managed to wrangle a compromise out of the people. They would have their services and observe the Sabbath until the noon hour. Then they would harness the wagons and move on.

"Think you can find us a place half a day on, Mister Calhoun?" Coldhammer asked. He was trying to keep the anger and bitterness out of his voice.

"I reckon," Calhoun snapped. He was not happy with this turn of events. He vowed that it would not become a regular occurrence. He had nothing against God or the Sabbath, but he did have experience out here. On this trail, stopping one day out of seven could be dangerous, possibly fatal.

Still angry, Calhoun pulled himself onto his skewbald horse and rode out of camp, leaving a bitter, sour group of travelers behind.

Just about the time he figured the wagon train was getting to a start, he found a campsite he thought would serve. He unsaddled his horse, made a small fire, and heated a pot of coffee.

An hour or so later, he shot a deer that had come down to the water to drink. It would be good eating, but he found himself eager to be out a little farther. They would be entering real buffalo country soon. Then these pilgrims would see about good eating, he thought.

Just before dark, the wagons began clanking into view. Calhoun smiled sourly. He was often perverse and did things to confound people. He had managed to fend off even more complaints by having gathered enough firewood for all the wagons.

In another display of perversity, Calhoun set a punishing pace the next day, forcing the people to travel much faster than they desired. The grumbling, which he had manage to dissipate a little with his gathering of firewood the night before, returned quickly. The day after and the day after that were more of the same.

Calhoun could not hear the complaints, though, traveling far out ahead of the first wagon as he was. Even if he could hear it, he would not have cared.

Coldhammer, however, had to listen to it close up.

Once again he used all the diplomacy he could muster to keep the people from revolting. He was not the kind of man to want to use force, but he finally had to resort to chaining one hothead to a wagon wheel for the night to cool him off some.

The wagon master wanted to speak to Calhoun about it, but he had learned right off that Calhoun was not an easy man to approach. In fact, the saddle tramp was damned near impossible to approach. So Coldhammer put it off and fretted.

While Calhoun could not hear the grumbling, he was aware of it. He knew the travelers were talking about the harshness of the trip. But he didn't give a hoot. He just went about his business in his own way. He knew, though, that it was only a matter of time before someone called him on it.

A little more than a week after leaving St. Joseph, the wagon train had reached the Platte River. Calhoun had, as usual, found them a good campsite. The river was moving sluggishly, but it provided good water. There was wood aplenty.

As the camp was being made, Calhoun laid out his bedroll away from the other people, as was his way. He tended the horse.

When he finished, he walked slowly through the heavy darkness toward Coldhammer's fire. Despite Calhoun's standoffishness, he had been eating his breakfast and supper with the wagon master and his family daily.

The meals were uncomfortable for Coldhammer and his family, and Calhoun took a perverse pleasure in irritating the wagon master.

The only one of the Coldhammers who did not seemed disturbed at his presence was the daughter, Polly. Indeed, she even seemed to look forward to Calhoun's twice-daily visits.

As he passed one of the other fires, around which six men sat, he overheard a bit of their talk. It was the mention of his name—attached to several epithets—that really caught his attention.

CHAPTER

* 6 *

Calhoun stopped in the shadows outside the orange ring of firelight and listened.

The six men were among the few whom he had tried to remember during the introductions that first day. They looked tough. Calhoun was not afraid of them—he was not afraid of anything that walked, crawled, swam or slithered—but he had suspected they might be trouble. Though they had tried nothing in the little more than a week the wagon train had been on the trail, Calhoun never doubted that feeling.

Now, listening to the six talking around the fire, he was certain.

One, a brutish bull of a man whom Calhoun recalled was named Rollie Pepperdine, was saying, " . . . and I don't like his goddamn attitude. Swaggerin' son of a bitch."

"Me neither," another said.

Calhoun tried to put a name to the barely seen face and the thin voice. He finally did. The small, undergrown runt of a man was aptly named Tiny Bates.

"Damn him. Ridin' 'roun' wit' all them big guns on his fancy-ass saddle. Geez," Bates added.

"I say we stomp his ass into the ground straight off and let him know he ain't the boss 'round here," Bass Cutler growled.

Cutler was easy for Calhoun to identify. He was about five-foot-eight and weighed at least three hundred pounds. His voice was breathless-sounding, as if it was having trouble squeezing out through the layers of lard.

"You others agree?" Pepperdine asked.

With his size and seeming fierceness, it was apparent to Calhoun that the others looked at him as something of a leader.

"He looks kind of mean to me," another man said. His voice wasn't quite a whine, but a strong under-current of perpetual fear always ran through it.

It took Calhoun a moment to place a name—Chuck Dillard—to the man. Except for the nasally voice, he was nondescript in size and looks.

"Shoot," Pepperdine snarled. He hawked up some phlegm and spit into the fire. Then he took a slurp of coffee before he continued. "I 'spect Tiny here could take him hisself. But if it'll make you feel better, Chuck, I'll see to it my own self."

"I'll help," Bates interjected. There was more than a tinge of eager dementia to his voice.

"If I get hard-pressed, I'll call on you," Pepperdine said with a rumbling chuckle. He was quite fond of Bates, liking the edge of mental instability the man carried like a badge.

"When're you gonna go after him, Rollie?" Billy Quince asked.

Quince was the most normal-looking of the men.

He was a handsome young man with shaggy mustache, curly hair, and piercing brown eyes.

"When the time's right, Billy. When the time's right," Pepperdine said, apparently trying to sound both ominous and mysterious.

"How's about now?" Calhoun asked in a soft growl. He swaggered into the firelight.

Six pairs of eyes turned on him with varying expressions. Dillard's held fear; Bates's fanaticism; Cutler's interest, as if he saw Calhoun as a specimen of some kind; Pepperdine's with expectation.

"I suppose that'd do," Pepperdine said quietly.

He set down his tin mug and started to push himself up, grinning at his companions.

Pepperdine was about halfway up when Calhoun kicked him in the jaw.

Pepperdine grunted in surprise and pain. He fell to the side, landing heavily atop Tiny Bates.

The scrawny little man squawked as he was buried under the huge Pepperdine.

"Hey, goddamnit," Cutler snapped, trying to shove his fat-laced carcass up. As usual, even such a simple-seeming maneuver was giving him trouble.

Calhoun smashed Cutler in the face with a hard left fist, followed immediately by a harder right.

Cutler was knocked back down on his rump. Blood ran from his nose.

Billy Quince suddenly surged upward to his feet, and headed at Calhoun low, looking to tackle him around the legs. He figured that if he could bring Calhoun down, he and the others would have little trouble finishing him off.

Calhoun took two swift steps up and out of the way. He spun, his knuckles cracking sharply across Quince's temple as he backhanded the charging man.

Quince grunted and sprawled on the ground.

Calhoun stamped his boot down on Quince's back, where it joined the neck, flattening him face-down in the dirt.

Quince moaned, and he went limp. All the fight fled from him in a hurry.

Pepperdine was on his feet now. He rubbed a beefy hand across his jaw. Nothing was broken, but it hurt like hellfire.

He glared at Calhoun, wanting to disparage Calhoun's courage for having attacked him unsuspecting like that. He had enough sense to know, however, that he would be laughed at, not only by Calhoun, but also his companions and most likely everyone else in the wagon train who heard about it.

He spit, then charged.

Calhoun had whirled and was waiting. He knew taking Pepperdine down again would not be as easy as before. Not when the big, burly man was on his guard.

Pepperdine ran into Calhoun, and the two men grappled, muscles straining.

The other five men were silent as Calhoun and Pepperdine fought quietly, each sweating and looking for something to gain a slight advantage over the other.

Some of the other men from the wagon train began gathering in a quiet circle. Only a few of the travelers were venturesome enough to place a few small wagers among themselves.

The two men struggled in silence.

At one point, Calhoun became dimly aware that the sixth man who had been at the fire, Sherman North, was creeping up behind him. As North swung his arm up—and Calhoun noticed he had a good-size log in hand—Calhoun took a step back and shoved Pepperdine with all his strength, spinning him around.

North managed to jerk his arm so the log went wide of his friend. Calhoun spit at him over Pepperdine's shoulder.

Calhoun and Pepperdine began to struggle anew. Pepperdine's size began to win out, though. He eventually was able to fling Calhoun to the ground.

Calhoun hit and rolled, dust flying up. Pepperdine whirled around like a caged bear and lashed out with a foot.

Calhoun grunted as Pepperdine's boot caught him in the ribs, increasing the speed of his rolling.

Pepperdine stalked after Calhoun, who finally came to a stop against a cowering Chuck Dillard. Pepperdine kicked again, his boot grazing Calhoun's head. He went to kick out again, but Calhoun was waiting and caught Pepperdine's foot.

Holding the appendage, Calhoun scrabbled up. When he was on his feet, Calhoun wrenched Pepperdine's foot viciously.

Pepperdine howled as the ligaments in his ankle stretched and twisted. Calhoun let go of the foot.

Pepperdine, who was off balance, fell heavily. He

landed on his side and clutched his right ankle with both hands. A moan escaped his lips.

Calhoun swept Pepperdine's companions with his eyes. Quince was still lying with his face down; Cutler and Bates looked stunned, and Dillard appeared to be ready to vomit with fear. North, a grizzled, wiry, mean-looking old coot, simply sat, glaring at Calhoun with piggish little eyes.

Calhoun turned back toward Pepperdine. The big man had gotten up and was standing precariously on his one good leg. He was reaching for his holstered sidearm.

"Don't," Calhoun warned.

Pepperdine froze, hand suspended over the gun butt. He tested his twisted ankle and found it would hold him. It wasn't perfect, but it would do for now. He smiled viciously at Calhoun. "Best say your final prayers, boy, if you know any."

Calhoun said nothing. He just took three quick steps, and snapped two quick punches at Pepperdine's face before the big man could react. Pepperdine shuffled back under the blows, feeling his ankle giving way again. He fought for balance.

Calhoun kicked Pepperdine in the right knee. Pepperdine's leg collapsed, and he went down onto the injured knee. He looked up in time to see Calhoun's hard right fist just before it exploded against his nose. The camp spun before his eyes, and then he was swept up by an overwhelming blackness.

"Anybody else?" Calhoun asked.

He was barely breathing hard despite the effort. He looked around the circle of people.

Pepperdine's cronies seemed quite unwilling to help him. The others of the wagon train, men, some women, and a few children, stood watching. Their faces betrayed their wonder at what had just transpired in their midst.

Calhoun knew he would have more trouble with Pepperdine and the big man's five cronies. The thought did not worry him, though. He figured he would handle it when it arose. Even if he paid the ultimate price for it—something he had given more than a little thought to—he would take at least a couple of the bastards with him when he went. He was absolutely sure of that.

He would, he knew, just have to be a bit more wary than he usually was. Since being cautious was almost second nature to him anyway, it would make little difference in the way he lived.

Calhoun brushed himself off, picked up his hat, and walked to Coldhammer's fire.

Under the wagon master's baleful gaze, Calhoun allowed Coldhammer's nubile young daughter, Polly, to fill his plate with beans and bacon and biscuits. He let his coffee cup be filled, and he moved off a few yards. He sat with his back against the wheel of a big wagon. That way he could keep an eye on most of the camp and still be fairly assured that no one could sneak up on him.

Coldhammer strolled up to Calhoun, trying to look nonchalant. But he could not hide his discomfort. He squatted in front of Calhoun.

"Evenin', Mister Calhoun," the wagon master said. He was unable to disguise his uneasiness.

Calhoun ignored him.

The silence between the two men deepened until it was thicker than week-old coffee.

Finally Coldhammer pushed himself up. The move was accompanied by assorted noises associated with creaking bones and a man beginning to feel his nearly fifty years more than he should, or wanted.

Coldhammer walked stiffly away, feeling like an idiot. He knew he had to talk to Calhoun—not only about what had just transpired, but also about what had gone on since they had left St. Joseph. He could not force the hard-edged Wade Calhoun into talking.

Still, he realized that the situation would only become worse if it was not addressed soon. He vowed to take another stab at it tomorrow. He did not relish the thought in the least.

Calhoun knew what Coldhammer was thinking, but he had no pity for the wagon master. Coldhammer would have to wrestle with his own demons. Calhoun had enough of his own plaguing him; he could not afford sympathy for another.

He finished eating and brought the plate, mug, knife, and fork to the Coldhammer fire. He handed them to Polly.

The golden-haired young woman smiled shyly at Calhoun. The look offered infinite promise.

It stirred Calhoun. His hard, pocked face eased minutely, and the thin, cruel lips curled up fractionally at the ends.

"Obliged, Miss Polly," he growled. "For the vittles, and for your services."

"My pleasure, Mister Calhoun." Polly's smile widened, and the promise for Calhoun deepened with it.

He took note of it as he strolled away. Tomorrow, he promised himself, he would make a frontal assault on Miss Polly Coldhammer. She was, he decided, a woman worth conquering.

CHAPTER

* 7 *

Barrett Coldhammer didn't get a chance to talk with Calhoun. Actually, though he would not admit it, he made little effort to talk with the guide the next day. Or the day after, or any time soon.

Coldhammer was not, by nature, a timid fellow, but Wade Calhoun was a more formidable man than he had ever encountered before. He didn't like the feeling of intimidation Calhoun produced in him, and that bothered him.

He figured he would have to have some kind of confrontation with Calhoun sooner or later. The situation with the travelers was growing more and more tense. The emigrants were unhappy, and growing more so with each passing day.

Coldhammer was becoming concerned that the people would revolt and cast him out as captain. He wouldn't mind so much being relieved of the onerous duty, but it would cut him to the quick to be considered not up to the job by the others.

Putting it off, though, seemed to be the best thing, or so Coldhammer tried to convince himself. However, such indecision frustrated him.

The wagon master also watched with growing

irritation as his daughter showed more and more affection for Calhoun. He fumed and fussed about it, but there was really nothing that he could do. He could not even really mention it to Polly.

Calhoun had made no attempt that Coldhammer could tell to seduce Polly. Indeed, Calhoun had been his usual self around Polly, gruff but always polite and well within the bounds of civility.

Coldhammer knew that short of shackling her in irons, there was nothing he could do to prevent Polly from forming an alliance with Calhoun should she choose to.

That was the main reason Coldhammer was so irritated, and he shuddered to even contemplate the possibility of Polly doing such a thing.

Calhoun knew what Coldhammer was thinking, and he became even more chummy with Polly, or as friendly as a solitary iconoclast like he could get. At all times, he still remained within the bounds of propriety.

He did it just to get Coldhammer's goat. It was another sign of his capricious sense of humor. The more Coldhammer grew irritated at it, the more Calhoun tried to get on the wagon master's nerves.

Calhoun knew that Polly was more than a little interested in him. He also figured that she most likely would be more than willing to bed down with him, if he but asked.

He held back, though. Not that he didn't enjoy thinking of the possibilities offered by a tryst with Polly Coldhammer. It was because of her father that Calhoun hesitated.

Calhoun might have an odd sense of humor and silently enjoy the consternation he produced in Coldhammer with it. However, he had realized he didn't want to hurt the wagon master. He wasn't sure why. It wasn't friendship with Coldhammer; he had not had any real friends in years.

He finally decided it was more a case that he didn't *dislike* the wagon master rather than liking him. Coldhammer was seemingly the only voice of reason and sanity—besides his own, of course—in the caravan.

While he figured it interesting and fun to tease and try to irritate Coldhammer, Calhoun did not necessarily want to take advantage of the man. Or at least any more than was necessary.

So, he confined his attentions to Polly to an occasional comment or a frequent look of interest. Those things were just enough to pique Polly's interest, and Coldhammer's annoyance.

The woman who did catch his eye—and occupied his more serious thoughts of lusty abandon—was the only other attractive, single young woman along with the wagon train: Erline Rae North, the daughter of Sherman North.

Erline Rae was fairly tall and willowy, though still fully curvaceous. She usually had a slightly sardonic smile curling her full, red lips and a lustful excitement in her smoky gray eyes. Her skin was a creamy olive.

From experience, Calhoun knew Erline Rae was not innocent. She had the look about her of a woman who was used to dealing with all kinds of men and had no real interest in settling down with one man. At least not yet. All that was encouraging to Calhoun.

Erline Rae was quite the opposite of Polly Coldhammer. Polly might try to look the wanton wench, but she really was innocent of men. Deep down, she also wanted nothing more than to marry a good man.

That, as much as anything else, had turned Calhoun away from trying to encourage Polly's attentions more than was necessary to amuse her and to irritate her father.

Erline Rae, on the other hand, was open and inviting and not set on landing a man permanently. She was a woman who would be satisfied with a good time, and Calhoun was sure he could provide her with that. The thoughts encouraged Calhoun to set his sights in Erline Rae's direction.

Still, he had held off, waiting to see the lay of things, before he moved on her. Especially after his altercation with her father and his friends. Calhoun figured that such a thing might easily turn Erline Rae against him; it would so with many women.

Calhoun found, though, that his concerns were unfounded. He also learned that he need not have taken so much patience with, or wasted so much time before pursuing, Erline Rae. It was she who made the first move.

She came to him quietly in the dead of the night after they had been on the trail almost two weeks. She almost died for her efforts.

Wade Calhoun was a man who had lived with danger all his life. He long ago had become accustomed to coming awake fast and fully alert, usually with one of his big pistols in hand. It was another of the reasons he had survived.

He reacted in just such a way when Erline Rae walked up to his bedroll. His camp was, as usual, set off a little apart from that of the other travelers. It also was shielded from the main group by several small cottonwood trees.

He had popped awake at the slight sound. He rolled out of the blankets and stood in one move. He had a Dragoon in his right hand. Almost instinctively he had leveled the pistol at the newcomer's breast. The hammer was cocked and his finger ready to apply the slight pressure needed to fire the big revolver.

Calhoun managed to restrain himself in that half a heartbeat before the pistol flashed and roared.

He sucked in a harsh, rattling breath and eased the hammer down.

Erline Rae stood there in her nightdress. One hand was pressed to her bosom, which heaved spasmodically in surprise. Her mouth formed a circle and her dark eyes were wide with fright. She knew exactly how close she had just come to death.

The smoldering desire bit deep inside her again once the Colt pistol was back in Calhoun's holster. He had spun and slid the holstered revolver under the blanket that he was using as a pillow.

Erline Rae smiled crookedly. She was still frightened, but she was determined not to let it stop her. Besides, the heat of her desire was burning away the last remnants of fear.

"If y'all didn't want me to come 'round to see y'all, Mister Calhoun," she said in a voice tinged with the soft tones of magnolia, "all you had to do was jus' say so."

She giggled softly and only a little self-consciously. She was glad it was dark, too, since it hid the blush of embarrassment. The feeling surprised her. She usually did not experience such timidity, or whatever it was that had suddenly caught her up.

"Fool," Calhoun muttered beneath Erline Rae's hearing.

Aloud, he said politely, "Sneakin' up on a man like that's a good way to get killed, ma'am." The warning was evident, though veiled.

"I know," Erline Rae whispered. Fear knotted up her belly again, and she fought against it.

"What're you doin' here anyway?" Calhoun asked. He thought he knew, but wanted to be sure.

Erline Rae's confidence began returning. She always felt on top of the situation when things turned this way. Men, she figured, were so predictable at such times.

"And just why do you think, Mister Calhoun?" she asked in a throaty voice. She smiled softly at him in the moonlight. "I'd think a man of your experience would know that."

"I do," Calhoun said only a little harshly. "I just wanted to make sure you did, too."

"Oh, I'm sure." Erline Rae said. Her voice dripped with desire. She was confident and self-assured once again, all her fear having fled. "I know exactly what I'm—"

"This ain't no time for talkin'," Calhoun said roughly.

He swept Erline Rae into his arms. His mouth sought hers.

She responded willingly, excited by this hard, strong, almost handsome saddle tramp.

As she had known it would, the situation these past few seconds with Calhoun had been so much different from such a time ever was with the huge, brutish Rollie Pepperdine, or fat, odorous Bass Cutler, or the demonically leering Tiny Bates, or any of the others.

Erline Rae didn't mind so much that her father "encouraged" her to spread her favors among his friends. It had been going on for so long that she hardly knew better. She wished, though, that just once in a while he—or they—would take her feelings and needs into account. They never did, however, though it had not stopped her from seeking someone on her own who would do that.

She could tell by Calhoun's short, hungry kiss that he certainly would.

Calhoun broke off the kiss, bent, and scooped Erline Rae up. She was surprised a little by the strength in his arms. He was so thin, with a razor-sharp face, that it did not seem he could be so strong. She enjoyed learning it, though.

Calhoun knelt and eased her down on the rough bedroll made of blankets and canvas.

Erline Rae looked up at him with lust smoldering in her gray eyes. That was evident in the light of the half-moon.

With a few swift, sure movements, she had worked the nightdress off and tossed it aside.

Calhoun looked down at her appreciatively before standing and shucking his clothes.

Then he was stretched out beside her on the blankets, feeling her warm flesh quivering against his.

Erline Rae's visits to Calhoun became a regular—though not nightly—occurrence.

She had considered going to him every night but then decided against it. One reason was that her father all too often made other arrangements for her with Pepperdine or one of the others. Those times were becoming more distasteful for her, now that she had been with Calhoun, but there was nothing she could do to get out of them.

Another reason was her reluctance to spend each night with him. She thought that irregular visits, rather than frequent ones, would do more to keep Calhoun's interest in her at a fever pitch.

It would be at least another two months until they hit Oregon, and she wanted to keep Calhoun interested in her at least that long. After that, she would have a whole new territory to explore.

Calhoun enjoyed the visits, but he did not sit and pine for Erline Rae when she did not show up. Nor did he wait for her expectantly. He simply went to sleep when he was tired.

After that first time, she had learned to arrive at a little earlier hour, before he would have turned in.

She had no hankering to be shot down by an awakening Wade Calhoun.

Calhoun did not place any significance on the visits. He took them for what they were—good times with a lusty, unattached, attractive female.

Erline Rae saw them similarly, and Calhoun knew that. He also knew she was using him to some extent, but he didn't mind. It was not a one-sided thing by any means.

CHAPTER
* 8 *

The wagon train inched along, making twenty or thirty miles one day, maybe ten the next. One of the toughest parts was through the sand hills along the Platte River in the area that would, in a decade or more, become Nebraska.

As he had since the beginning, though, Calhoun kept the people on the trail for long hours every day. The emigrants complained vociferously for a while.

Their complaints lessened a little after the travelers had passed two other, much larger wagon trains. It made them feel they were really getting somewhere. Besides, they would have a better choice of campsites now, as well as better hunting and cleaner water.

Once they had passed the real sand hill area, they hit prime buffalo country. They had encountered herds of the big shaggies before on the trail, but now the herds were immense. The brown, bulky bodies frequently spread out for miles in all directions, slowing the wagon train's progress, and, once, even bringing it to a halt.

This, however, was also the land which the Sioux, Cheyenne, Pawnee, Kaw, and Crow and other warlike tribes hunted in and fought over.

Calhoun could not believe the good fortune that had ridden with the wagon train for the first several weeks. They had seen few Indians, and had encountered only minor troubles.

That began to change, though, as they rolled along the wide, muddy, shallow Platte River.

Their first encounter with Indians came when a small band of Pawnees showed up.

The Indians, too few in number to attack the wagons, had instead tried to get some presents from the travelers. They rode up close to the wagons, scowling and looking fiercely at the white travelers.

Coldhammer had enough sense to get most of the women inside the wagons, behind the tarps, so they would not be harassed by the warriors.

Then he tried to talk with the seven wild-looking warriors. He seemed to make no progress, though, and grew frustrated rapidly.

The warriors sneered at Coldhammer, and at the rest of the white travelers. They were unimpressed with these drifting white-eyes. Only the threat of so many rifles and pistols aimed at them kept them from attacking.

The Pawnees were getting more insistent, and increasingly nasty. Their mostly bald heads, broken only by a greased strip of hair longitudinally down the center, gleamed in the day's sunlight. Their polished bronze chests and arms rolled with sweat.

Coldhammer was nervous as he turned his back on the Indians. He rode slowly back toward the wagons, which had stopped.

"Move on out again," Coldhammer roared, trying

to ignore the Indians behind him. He knew that to show any of the fear he felt would doom him and most likely precipitate a bloodbath.

"But, Cap'n," the man in the lead wagon protested.

"Don't but me, Lije Wilkins," Coldhammer snapped. "You just go and do as you're told."

Wilkins looked pasty with fear as he faced the front and slapped the long reins on the backs of the mules. Wilkins was one of the few travelers with this group whose wagon was pulled by mules. Most of the others were hauled by oxen, with the people walking alongside, or behind, the wagon.

As the wagons began to plod ahead, the warriors rushed forward and swept in front of the lead wagon. They stopped there, in a short, bronze arc in front of the travelers.

Wilkins jerked on the reins, bringing his ponderous wagon to a halt.

"Keep movin'!" Coldhammer bellowed, trotting his horse in that direction. "Damnit, Lije, move!"

With a look of decided reluctance, Wilkins once again snapped the reins. The big wagon lurched forward a few feet as the mules strained at the harness. Then it moved more smoothly, though certainly slowly, toward the phalanx of grim Pawnee warriors.

Wilkins began having second, third, and even fourth thoughts in the few yards before the lead mules' muzzles were pushing into the group of warriors. He was not happy with this maneuver, and he regretted having insisted upon being the lead wagon. At his advanced age, he did not need troubles such as these.

He grew even more worried and afraid when he noticed that one Pawnee had leveled a rifle at him. Two others had nocked arrows. Wilkins began to sweat. He considered stopping the wagon, Barrett Coldhammer be damned.

Suddenly Wade Calhoun appeared alongside Wilkins's team, seemingly out of nowhere.

"Whoa up, mules," Wilkins called, tugging on the reins. Relief flooded through him. The wizened old man never had taken much of a liking to Calhoun, but he was sure glad as hell to see the guide now.

Calhoun had been several miles out ahead of the caravan, prowling, as he usually did. Many of the travelers thought he did nothing, but there was more to his roaming than met the eye.

He was constantly on the alert for Indian sign. He could not be everywhere, of course, but he usually traveled in a wide curve out in front of the wagons. It allowed him to view the most territory as he could without having to circle the wagons.

He also hunted; marked the trail, which often did not directly follow a river or stream; sought campsites; plotted the next day's march; made sure the trail wasn't bringing them through too large a buffalo herd, and more.

Calhoun did not know what made him turn back. He operated so often on instinct and reflex that he frequently had no idea of how he knew things. Like now. He had seen no sign of Indians; but he somehow just knew that there were some about. Since they were on the south side of the Platte, they were in Pawnee country. He figured it was them.

He was just as certain that the Indians were near the wagon train. He didn't question such thoughts; he just acted on them. He spun his skewbald horse and rode hellbent on his back trail.

He had topped a small rise and began plunging down the far slope when he first saw the wagons— and the group of Pawnee warriors—just to the north. He slowed immediately, trying to take in the entire scene, learn what was happening.

He spun and raced eastward. A quarter of a mile away, he swung northward again, and then a little later, back west, toward the wagons.

He came up on the wagons from the north side, between the wagons and the river. Most of the folks were so intent on fearfully watching the Indians that they did not see Calhoun until he was easing up along the right side of Lije Wilkins's wagon.

He called for the mules to stop, with their snouts almost touching Pawnee flesh.

Calhoun moved up alongside the mules and stopped a few feet away from the warriors. Hate and anger burned in his chest as he thought back a few years.

He pushed those thoughts away. They had no place here, now.

Calhoun waved a hand in the vague direction of the Pawnees' weapons. "You boys don't need those things," he said easily. Though he spoke calmly, quietly, his face was as hard as stone.

The Indians made no move of any kind. They just

sat there staring blankly at Calhoun, their faces every bit as hard as his.

"I said, you boys don't need them weapons," Calhoun repeated slowly.

The Pawnees might not know too much English, but Calhoun was certain they knew at least some. They lived too near the settlements to not have learned some.

Still the warriors said or did nothing.

Calhoun slowly wrapped his reins around the huge saddlehorn of his fancy saddle. When he finished, his right hand moved easily until it was resting lightly on one of the big Colt Walkers in the saddle holster. He stared at the Indians, as unblinking as they.

Finally one tall, potbellied Pawnee made a short, chopping motion with one hand. The warrior who had the rifle uncocked it and raised the barrel skyward. The warrior rested the butt of the rifle on his thigh.

The other two unnocked their arrows, but kept them at the ready. The three other Pawnees still had not moved.

"You're on Pawnee land," the potbellied one said in heavily accented English.

"The Sioux might think otherwise in these parts," Calhoun said with a slight smirk.

The Pawnee war chief glared, and his patrician nose twitched with anger. "I am Blood Runs," he snarled, as if the name and his tones were sufficient to inspire fear. "And this is my land."

"And what if it is?" Calhoun seemed unconcerned.

"I am Blood Runs!" the Pawnee roared. "Only by my word will you be allowed to pass!" His accent made the words difficult to understand, but the meaning was clear.

So was Calhoun's. "Buffalo shit," he sneered.

A gasp of frightened surprise sprang up behind Calhoun. In front of him, the Pawnees stared at him with varying degrees of hate, anger, or shock.

"It's only through my good heart that y'all ain't been killed yet," Calhoun added. His voice still rang with conceit.

Blood Runs was nearly beside himself with anger, though he kept himself in check. Calhoun could see it in the warrior's eyes, though.

"Now, Blood Runs, how's about you and your shit-smellin' *compadres* there turn 'round and haul your asses back to whatever sorry village you call home." It was not a question.

Blood Runs fought against his rage.

The Pawnees jabbered among themselves for a few minutes in their own language. Through it all, Calhoun did not move, other than to turn his head to the left when he caught a movement there.

Barrett Coldhammer had ridden up along the other side of Wilkins's mules and stopped even with Calhoun. He nodded nervously at Calhoun. The guide responded in kind and then turned back to face the Indians.

After several more minutes' discussion, Blood Runs looked at Calhoun. He appeared to have regained some of his reason.

"You are not fit to raid," he said in his garbled

English. "You have too few horses. And those are no more than wolf bait."

"So?" Calhoun asked. Though he had spoken nonchalantly, he was relieved. He had no real desire to force a battle with these Pawnees.

While the travelers might outnumber the Indians considerably, few, if any, of the emigrants had experience fighting Indians. It would be a bloody, devastating battle, if it came. He was glad to see that the Pawnees were exhibiting little desire to fight either.

"So," Blood Runs added, "we will let you pass."

Calhoun could hear a sigh of relief go up from the people behind him, but he knew it would not be quite so easy.

"And what would you want to let us pass through the land of Blood Runs?" Calhoun asked.

The Pawnee shrugged. To ask for things would be akin to begging. Blood Runs was too proud for that. He wanted this sharp-eyed, hard-looking white man to make an offer. He also hoped it was a good one.

Calhoun nodded, figuring what the warrior was thinking. Without looking at the wagon master, Calhoun said, "Mister Coldhammer, have someone fetch up a couple bolts of cloth. Blue and red would be best."

Coldhammer had little experience in these matters, but he instinctively knew what was going on. More important, he understood why. "Anything else?" he asked.

"A sack of coffee, and two of sugar, if you can afford 'em. Maybe a couple mirrors or other such doodads as you have handy."

Coldhammer nodded. He slowly turned his horse, not wanting to make the Indians nervous. He rode back along the wagons, moving unhurriedly. About halfway back, he stopped at a wagon. For a moment, it looked like Reese Waymer, who owned the wagon, was going to argue.

A glance up at the Indians, though, and another at Coldhammer's tight face convinced him to back off.

He culled out the supplies he was ordered to get, though he grumbled the whole time about it.

Coldhammer took the items in his arms, balancing them and the reins at the same time. He rode back toward the Pawnees, still not showing any haste.

Though he was not looking at Coldhammer, Calhoun knew the wagon master was taking it slow and easy.

Calhoun was surprised at Coldhammer for having seen the wisdom of doing it. Not only would it be likely to keep the Indians peaceful by not making any sudden moves, it also would show the Pawnees that the travelers could not be hurried by threats. It was a good signal to send to these Indians, Calhoun decided.

Coldhammer gingerly eased up toward Blood Runs. He was nervous as could be but trying not to show it.

Blood Runs nodded to a warrior on his right. The Pawnee war chief was not to be outdone by the whites. If their leader did not fetch the gifts, Blood Runs would not accept them. The seconds would do the work that chiefs would not do.

The indicated warrior took the proffered items one at a time. He passed all but the bolt of red cloth to others. Each Indian who received a gift—and they all got something—yipped in victory.

"Y'all got your presents now . . ." Calhoun said after the few small things had been passed around. He did not have to finish the sentence. What he had said, and his look, were enough to send the Pawnees on their way.

"All right," Calhoun said, looking at Coldhammer, "let's move 'em out." He rode on ahead once more.

Coldhammer watched as the solitary figure dwindled with the distance. He was not quite sure of what to make of Wade Calhoun.

CHAPTER
* 9 *

Five days later, they faced a larger band of Sioux.

Calhoun had been more than two miles ahead of the wagons. He had spotted a drifting cloud of dust. It could be from a buffalo herd, he knew, or another wagon train, or Indians. It had to be checked out.

He rode to a nearby grassy swell. At the bottom, he hastily hobbled the horse with a short piece of rope. He loosened the saddle, and then walked up the knoll. About three-quarters of the way up, he flopped down and half crawled the rest of the way.

At the crest, he crept carefully over and stopped, lying along the top. He looked out, eyes sweeping the rolling landscape.

He spotted a small herd of buffalo, and two small, swift-moving groups of antelope. He knew that even together, all three groups could not have produced the dust cloud he had seen.

He continued his scanning. Within a moment, he had found the cloud of dust. It was moving from northwest to southeast coming at a diagonal from his left. He nodded.

Standing, Calhoun walked down the hill. He

grabbed a few pieces of buffalo jerky and his canteen. Then he strolled back up the rise and sat. He munched on jerky and sipped from the canteen as he waited.

The dust cloud proceeded slowly, almost majestically, but steadily.

Calhoun realized after a while that the cloud—and whatever had caused it—would not pass too closely. He wasn't sure yet whether to be relieved or not. There was still every chance it was made by a buffalo herd.

He didn't think that was the case, though. It was moving too steadily to be something as capricious as a herd of buffalo. He suspected it was made by Indians. If that were true, it would seem that there was a heap of warriors, judging by that hanging swirl of dust.

Calhoun had long since finished his jerky and several cigarettes when the source of the dust came into view. Calhoun's face tightened as he spotted the warriors about a half-mile off. Even at that distance, he could tell they were Sioux. Just the thought of that name set his blood boiling.

He watched for a little while, trying to judge where they were heading in relation to the wagons. It became apparent soon enough that if the Sioux kept to their present course, they would run right into the caravan.

He half rolled partway down the knoll, not wanting to stand and skyline himself. He stood and walked hastily toward the horse. He tightened the cinch, hung the canteen on the saddle, and climbed onto the horse.

Calhoun wasted no time in his ride back to the wagons. He wanted to have time to prepare the travelers before the Sioux came upon them.

Barrett Coldhammer usually rode a horse, letting his wife or oldest child, Polly, crack the whip over the oxen that hauled their wagon. He figured that as wagon master, he should be mobile and ready for action.

It was Coldhammer's way to ride back and forth along the wagon train, offering encouragement where needed, help where necessary, advice when asked, and orders when called for. He wasn't sure, but he thought most of his charges felt the better for it.

He was so engaged when he saw a horseman galloping toward the wagons. It took him only a blink to realize that it was Calhoun. Worry clutched at Coldhammer's guts. Calhoun wouldn't be riding that way unless there was trouble. And trouble out here could mean only one thing.

"Damn," Coldhammer murmured. He spurred his horse and moved out quickly to meet Calhoun.

The two men pulled up near each other, horses breathing heavily.

"Sioux," Calhoun said simply.

Coldhammer nodded, fear tightening his sphincter. "Where?"

Calhoun pointed toward the northwest.

"How far?" Coldhammer's mouth was dry and his palms sweaty.

"Not far enough." Calhoun cast a glance back that

way. He half expected to see the Sioux come charging around a small, sandy knob. No one was there, though.

"We best get ready," he added.

"They lookin' to cause trouble?" Coldhammer's fear was palpable. It was surprising to him to realize that his fear now was far greater than when they had been so close to the Pawnees. Trouble was, he didn't know why, unless it was all those things he had heard about the savage Sioux Indians.

Calhoun shrugged. As far as he was concerned, the Sioux were born to cause trouble. To Calhoun, the Sioux were little more than devils on earth, fractious heathens who lived on blood and death. He knew that was not what Coldhammer had meant, though.

"I expect they ain't lookin' for it directly," Calhoun allowed. "But they'll sure as hell jump on it when they spot us."

"I was afraid of that." He paused a minute, chewing on the ends of his shaggy mustache.

"Fort them wagons up as best you can. Get the animals inside to protect 'em. Make sure the women and young 'uns are safe as they can be."

"And the men?"

"The men best be ready to spill some blood, Mister Coldhammer," Calhoun said sourly. He might like to kill Indians, especially Sioux, for what they had done to him, but he did not relish a fight with those Indians. The Sioux, as many other tribes, had earned his grudging respect. They were not a people to be trifled with.

Coldhammer nodded. "We'd best hurry, I'd suppose?"

"I'd recommend it."

Without another word, Coldhammer turned his horse and both men raced toward the wagons, which had crept closer while they had talked. They rode to each wagon, telling the driver, or the whip-cracker of the plan.

The travelers had been on the trail close to a month now, and they were used to working together. Forming a rough box of the wagons, with the horses, mules, and oxen inside, was a common nightly practice for them, so doing it quickly and surely was not difficult.

With swift certainly, the wagons were brought into place. As the men began herding the animals inside the makeshift fort, women gathered up children. A few women and all the children took shelter behind a hastily thrown-up shelter of equipment and furniture, near one side of the box.

A few of the younger men and some older boys stayed with the animals. They would work to keep the stock from bolting or causing too much consternation.

All the rest of the men began taking up positions under or behind wagons. Women stood by with powder horns and lead, ready to reload for husbands, brothers, or friends.

Martha Coldhammer took her place near her husband. Pride was reflected in her eyes as she watched him working or issuing orders.

Coldhammer was aware of it, but tried not to

think about it, lest he get too embarrassed to function properly.

As much as he hated to do it, too, he offered Polly's services as a reloader to Calhoun. There was, Coldhammer figured, no one else to do it.

Calhoun gruffly accepted. Polly smiled at him when he did that, but he hardly noticed. There was serious business to be taken care of here, and his mind was focused on that.

Finally all was ready, and none too soon.

To the emigrants, the Indians made a frightful spectacle when they rode into view around another of the interminable humps of land. They were a much more formidable-looking group than the Pawnees. It might have been because there were so many of them, compared with the small group of Pawnees. No one would attest to that, though.

"Hold your fire!" Calhoun yelled.

"Why?" someone shouted.

Calhoun had neither the time nor inclination to try to explain it to them. He didn't know the Sioux mind well, but he had dealt with them and other Indians before.

He figured the Sioux would make a pass at them, maybe two, trying to use their horses as shields, wanting to test the white men's defenses.

On the third or fourth pass, they would probably be riding straight up, taunting the whites, who were so afraid that they had to hide behind heavy wagons. Calhoun was hoping that the Sioux would be satisfied with that as a show of bravery. If so, they might take off without really challenging the entrenched force of better-armed whites.

"Just do what I said," he bellowed. He wanted to make sure everyone understood that. He thought they had a good chance of getting everyone through this alive, if a little patience was used.

The Sioux came at them as he had expected. The warriors howled and yelled, frightening more than a few of the travelers. They remained partially hidden though, firing arrows and guns from under their ponies' neck. The projectiles thudded harmlessly into the wood of the wagons.

To Calhoun's relief, and surprise, the men held their fire.

Suddenly the Sioux were gone, having raced over a ridge.

"Jesus," someone breathed behind Calhoun. His sentiments were echoed by several others.

Calhoun quickly spun and gave a hurried, shouted explanation of what he thought would happen next. Then he reissued his warning to hold fire until he gave the word.

Moments later, the warriors were thundering down on them again, screeching all the more.

Rollie Pepperdine stood up from behind his protection. "Hell, these savages ain't so bad," he bellowed, wanting to show off. He snapped his rifle up and squeezed off a shot.

"Damnit," Calhoun swore as he saw one of the warriors topple from his horse. He wondered whether the Sioux was alive. If he were, the Sioux might go easier on them all.

A moment later, the warrior stood. A companion swept down on him, an arm outstretched. The wounded Sioux grabbed the arm and swung up behind his companion as the horse continued racing along.

"Whoo-ee!" Pepperdine bellowed in victorious pride. "Showed them sons a bitches now, didn't I?"

A moment later, the Sioux charged with renewed fury. They came in a whirling flash of color, noise, dust, and arrow-punctuated violence.

Powder smoke clogged the air around the wagons, hanging in a sickly pall. Horses and mules bucked, trying to break free. Oxen lowed mournfully, too dumb to realize what was happening but knowing that their orderly little world had disappeared. Babies cried or screamed.

Though the whites were outnumbered, they were better armed and had the protection of the wagons. It was all that saved them.

The Sioux attacked again and again, racing around the wagons, trying to break through wherever an opportunity might blossom. After several minutes of attacking, they would flee toward one of the rises. After a tense wait, the attacks would come again.

During one of the headlong charges, something made Calhoun spin. He did so just in time to see a painted Sioux warrior leap his pony over a wagon tongue into the box of wagons. Just as his pony landed, the warrior jerked his lance forward, throwing it with all his might.

The lance plowed into the back of a young man

named Mike Wright. Wright's scream could not be heard above the din.

"Shit," Calhoun muttered. He whipped up the Dragoon in his right hand and fired the two balls remaining in it.

The Sioux hit the ground, bounced a few times, and then lay still. His creamy tan war shirt was covered with blood on the front and back.

Calhoun spun back and tossed the pistol to Polly. She caught it, almost dropping it. She reloaded it swiftly and surely and gave it back to Calhoun.

The Sioux attacked again and then disappeared once more. In the lull, Calhoun grabbed two nearby men and dragged them along. The three men grabbed the body of the Sioux that Calhoun had shot. Quickly they carried the body out of the enclosure and a short way across the plain, and set it down. Then they hurried back to their positions.

"What'n hell'd you do such a damnfool thing for?" Tiny Bates asked.

People looked expectantly at Calhoun. He didn't feel like answering, but he figured they wouldn't be satisfied unless he said something.

"These Injins'll go to any length to get back their dead and wounded," Calhoun said loudly enough for all to hear. "I expect you'd all rather have them get that one out there than in here."

Calhoun fumed as he stood at his post. Not only for everything that had happened so far, but also because he could hear Pepperdine and his crew firing at the Sioux body and laughing with each successful hit.

Then the warriors came at them again. It seemed a halfhearted effort though. They scooped up their dead companion, made one more pass, and then headed away, whooping. They had suffered two dead and two wounded, as far as Calhoun could tell.

"Think they're gone for good?" Coldhammer asked nervously.

"I expect," Calhoun allowed.

CHAPTER

* 10 *

As soon as the Indians' dust was out of sight, moving rapidly off to the north, Calhoun stomped up to Pepperdine.

Without a word, he slammed the unsuspecting big man in the side of the head with his rifle butt.

"Don't ever cross me again," Calhoun snarled, looming over the spraddled, dazed Pepperdine.

Pepperdine shook his head to clear the cobwebs. "Go to hell, you Injun-lovin' riffraff," Pepperdine snapped. He got up, gingerly rubbing his already discoloring jaw.

If there was one thing Wade Calhoun was not, it was an Indian lover. No one could say that of him. Visions of a Kansas farmstead flickered in Calhoun's vision. They quickly dissolved into the picture of a smoldering farmhouse and plots of trampled crops. Near the house were two bloody, desecrated corpses, both female. One was an adult, the other an infant.

The specters of Calhoun's past burst into a blinding rage that surged up from the depths of his soul and exploded with a fury few men had ever seen, let alone experienced.

Calhoun had been holding his rifle in both hands. As his rage got the better of him, he flicked the rifle's butt out as hard as he could, almost unconscious of doing it. The butt plate of the Henry rifle slammed against the side of Pepperdine's skull. The rifle's stock cracked with the impact.

Calhoun tossed the weapon down angrily. Then he proceeded to beat the living tar out of Pepperdine.

The big, burly Pepperdine could put up only minimal resistance. The blow from the rifle butt had stunned him, disrupting his body's functioning. Because of that, his arms and legs would not work quite right. His defense was pitiful, and did nothing to slow the assault.

Calhoun had become a man possessed. He no longer was fighting the big, suddenly cowering man before him, but rather the demons of his own past and his own mind.

His ironlike fists flashed out again and again, each eliciting a grunt or moan of pain from Pepperdine.

Each blow produced a powerful feeling of satisfaction in Calhoun. There was no joy in the damage he was wreaking on another human being, really. Instead, it was satisfaction of relief. It was as if he could exorcise the evils within him by pounding something, or someone.

The other travelers stood around. Most were uneasy. They were afraid to do anything to stop this destruction, and they were held in thrall by Calhoun's demonic fury.

Coldhammer considered shooting Calhoun to end the merciless beating. It seemed the only way to stop it. He stalled and waited, though. He figured he still needed Calhoun as a guide.

He also thought, momentarily and with more than a little fright, that he was not at all sure even a bullet would be enough to stop Calhoun in this condition.

Then Coldhammer noticed that Tiny Bates and Billy Quince were bringing their pistols to bear on Calhoun. It was obvious that they were waiting only for any opening to blast Calhoun into eternity.

That was enough for Coldhammer. He waggled a finger at a few of the men on the wagon train, and nodded at Quince and Bates. Six men brought rifles up, aimed at Pepperdine's two cronies.

Bates, who was more than half crazy, sported a wild look in his eyes. He seemed about ready to take on all six men, and then anyone else who was around.

Quince, though, had some common sense. He holstered his pistol and then turned toward Bates. He spoke softly but urgently to the small man.

After a few moments, Bates returned his pistol to the holster and folded his arms across his scrawny chest. He glared from Calhoun to Coldhammer and back. Hate glazed his maniacal eyes.

Coldhammer calmly stared back, hoping that Calhoun would finish punishing Pepperdine. Then they could all get back on the trail. Though Coldhammer looked calm enough to the others, he was worried. Not only did he have to contend with Calhoun, he knew that Bates and the others would be out for him sooner or later.

He wondered if perhaps he had not made a mistake in stopping Quince and Bates from gunning Calhoun down. He half figured that the travelers could get along without a guide, maybe even hire one at Fort Laramie. Coldhammer was not so sure that Pepperdine's band of ruffians would allow the rest of the trip—which was not yet half over—to be made in relative peace.

Coldhammer sighed, wishing once again that he had not taken on this job. He turned his eyes back to the beating.

Eventually Calhoun began to wind down on his own. Whether he was tired or had just ran out of rage, no one was sure.

Finally, though, the rampaging fists slowed and then stopped.

Calhoun stood back, looking down at the bloody meat-pile that was Rollie Pepperdine. Calhoun was breathing hard. He hardly seemed to recognize the pulpy, bloody human being lying at his feet, or anyone else for that matter.

Calhoun's sensibilities began to return slowly, and he straightened. He looked down at his knuckles. They were bruised and split. A little blood seeped out from the cracks. He knew they would hurt like hell by that night, but he didn't care. Not while he was still fighting off the pictures of that burning Kansas farmstead. Besides, he had always had a high tolerance for pain. Injuries such as these were nothing to him.

He glared at Quince and Bates; then swung his gaze to Sherman North, Chuck Dillard, and Bass Cutler.

"Any of you others want to test me?" he asked, voice harsh with anger and rage.

Bates looked about ready to come against Calhoun, but some flickering spark of reason ignited in his dull brain. That dim flame kept him from moving.

"Then I'll tell y'all what I told your dimwitted *compadre* here: Don't ever cross me again. None of you." His eyes blazed hotly. "I'll plug any and all who's stupid enough to try me."

Still fighting the fury inside, Calhoun scooped up his rifle. He stalked off toward his splotchy-colored horse. Within moments he had tightened the cinch on the saddle. He shoved the cracked rifle into the saddle scabbard and pulled himself into the saddle.

With force of will, he kept his hand from shaking in rage as he rolled and lighted a cigarette. He walked the horse over to where the travelers still stood, looking dazed. First a fight with Sioux; then the maniacal fury of Wade Calhoun.

"Best bury Mister Wright, if you're of a mind to," Calhoun told Coldhammer. "Then get the folks movin'."

The wagon master nodded, seeing the wisdom of it. "What about Rollie?" he asked, rather afraid to even mention the big man's name to Calhoun after what had happened only moments ago.

Calhoun shrugged.

Coldhammer looked up at Calhoun, undecided.

"I reckon his friends'll tend to him," Calhoun said coldly. "Ain't nobody else will."

Coldhammer still looked undecided.

"I expect you don't want to wait around for them Sioux to come back for another try," Calhoun said evenly.

"Think they will?" Coldhammer asked. His nervousness renewed itself with a vengeance.

Calhoun looked at him, and then surveyed the crowd. His eyes were icy hard. Then he looked back at Coldhammer. He spoke to the wagon master, but he knew the others were listening intently.

"Was things normal, I'd say no," Calhoun said in harsh tones. "But after all the trouble that goddamn fool Pepperdine's caused . . ." He shrugged.

"What trouble?" Cutler asked. There was a sneer in his voice and on his lips. "All he did was try'n kill some of those savage devils before they killed us."

There were a few murmurs of assent, and Cutler looked mighty pleased with himself.

Cutler withered under Calhoun's glare, though. "First off, Mister Cutler," Calhoun said in a tone as dark and threatening as his look, "he shot down that Injin in cold blood. There was no call for that."

He paused and took another look around. He had regained the sympathy of the crowd. "And then you, him, and your idiot cronies went and filled that other dead warrior full of holes for no goddamn good reason."

"So?" Cutler asked sharply. He wanted the travelers back on his side again. "He was just a goddamn Injun."

Calhoun sighed. It never ceased to amaze him how stupid people could be. He had no liking for Indians; none at all. Not after what they had done to him. But he had enough sense to know that their ways were different from his; that while they might be savages, they had their own ways.

In learning at least some of those ways, Calhoun had added years to his life since he could predict what various tribes might do in certain circumstances. He didn't have to like Indians to want to understand some things about them.

"The Sioux don't take kindly to such a thing," Calhoun said. He was no calmer now than he had been a few minutes ago. "Had we just driven them off, they most likely wouldn't be back. Now, though . . ." He shrugged.

Cutler seemed to shrink into his fatness as the majority of the travelers glared at him.

Coldhammer nodded. Everything Calhoun had said was true enough, he figured.

There was a sudden flurry of activity, making it apparent to Coldhammer that the others realized it, too. Already several of the men were hurrying to hitch their teams to their wagons.

"Any others killed?" Calhoun asked.

Coldhammer shook his head. "Not that I know of. Just Mister Wright. Two others were hurt, but not bad. One of Gus Stewart's mules was killed."

Calhoun nodded, and turned his horse's head.

"Where're you gonna be, Mister Calhoun?" Coldhammer asked, squinting into the sun up at Calhoun.

Calhoun pointed with his left hand, his smoldering cigarette sending up curls of smoke from between index and middle fingers, toward the west.

"What about the Sioux?"

Calhoun shrugged. He was not worried about those Indians. He figured he could keep out of their way should the need arise.

He touched his heels to the horse's side and trotted away through a new gap in the wagons. He felt a
great need to be alone for a spell, far from these
benighted emigrants.

He rode out only about a mile and a half at a good
lope. He might not be afraid of the Sioux, but he
could see no good reason to tempt fate, either. He
finally pulled up, dismounted, and loosened the saddle. He hobbled the horse and hung a feed bag of
oats over the animal's snout.

Calhoun sat, pulling his rifle across his lap, checking it over. It wasn't as bad as he had originally
thought, but it would have to be repaired.

He growled in annoyance. It wasn't that he felt
bad about what he had done to Rollie Pepperdine; it
was more that he was disgusted any time he could
not control himself. He rolled and lit a cigarette and
puffed it as he watched a small herd of buffalo grazing a hundred yards off.

Finishing the cigarette, he stubbed it out in the
dirt. Most of the pain and anger had gone, except for
the dull ache inside that was always there. He had
learned to live with that. Calhoun tied a rawhide
thong around the cracked stock of his rifle. He was
of a mood for fresh buffalo meat. He only hoped the
rifle could withstand the blast.

The buffalo, downwind from Calhoun, were used
to him now. He raised the rifle and fired. A cow went
down in a flapping circus of legs. The strange activity
unnerved the other animals, who rumbled off
toward the northwest.

Calhoun cleaned the rifle, lubricated it with the

small vial of sperm whale oil, but did not reload it.
He shoved the weapon into the scabbard and tightened the saddle's cinch.

He pulled himself into the saddle. Judging that he
had maybe three hours of daylight left, he hurried
down and butchered out as much meat as he
thought the horse could carry.

He rode away, bloody buffalo meat dripping
down his horse's sides.

Behind him, a pack of wolves descended on the
buffalo carcass.

CHAPTER

✶ 11 ✶

Polly Coldhammer usually abhorred violence.

The beating that Wade Calhoun had given Rollie Pepperdine made her quake at the knees. It was a shock to her when she realized the quaking was not from fear; it had been from excitement. At that time, she felt more alive than she ever had in all her eighteen and a half years.

The episode had left Polly weak—and wanting Calhoun more than ever.

Calhoun had been, she had noticed, a little more withdrawn around her of late. She didn't know why, and that bothered her even more than the fact of his standoffishness itself.

Watching him ride away from the wagons, his back straight, she decided that she would change his new aloofness toward her. She was determined that she would make him want her. She wasn't sure how, exactly, but she thought she knew of one sure way.

That way would give her mother palpitations if Martha Coldhammer ever found out about it. Polly smiled to herself at that. She, of course, had no intention of letting her mother know that she had ever even had such a thought.

Her father's hoarse bellow, roaring that everyone should make ready to leave—and damned soon— shook her from her thoughts. She turned toward her wagon.

Then she saw Clair Wright, the new widow of Mike Wright. Though Clair was one of four pregnant women with the caravan, she did not show it yet. Only a few people knew about it.

Clair stood there, tears streaming down her face, as she watched three men digging a grave for her slain husband. She looked woefully forlorn.

Polly went to Clair, who was only a year or so older than she was. Polly put her arm around Clair's shoulders and tried as best she could to comfort her friend. Even with that, though, Polly could not put Calhoun out of her mind.

The funeral, such as it was, was short. The emigrants were too used to such things by now. People died every other day out here, or so it seemed. If not from their wagon train, then from another. They had passed graves by the dozen on the journey.

The travelers were also goaded by fear of the Sioux returning. That served to speed them up.

With three men working, the grave did not take long to dig. Wright's body was wrapped in the finest quilt the Wrights had. Then he was lowered into the hole. Coldhammer said a few words over the grave, and dirt was tossed in.

When that happened, Polly led Clair away, to her own wagon. They talked softly until the grave was filled and then covered with such rocks as could be found and a wooden cross pounded in.

Then Coldhammer gave the order to move out. Polly looked at her teary-eyed friend, and her heart went out to her. "You sure you can drive that wagon by yourself?" Polly asked anxiously.

Clair nodded. She blew her nose delicately and then dabbed at her eyes. She missed her husband of just over a year something terrible, but she knew that life had to go on. She straightened her back and nodded again, more firmly.

Polly was still dubious, but she accepted it. "You come callin' on me if you need anything, you hear," she said to Clair.

The widow nodded once more. Then she climbed up onto her wagon. Some of the men had hitched up her team for her. She sat, waiting for the signal to move.

Polly wandered back to her father's wagon. Despite her concern for her friend, she still could not get Calhoun out of her mind. Throughout the rest of that afternoon, as she strode purposefully along beside her plodding, ox-drawn wagon, she wondered about him. Though she had the rough outline of a plan in mind, she was not quite sure how to go about it. It sat on her mind all the time she was walking.

One of the problems she had was her clothes. She realized sometime during that afternoon that she was ashamed of how she was dressed. Her bonnet and plain linsey-woolsey dress were serviceable, even mostly presentable. But they sure as all get-out were not designed to attract a man. Especially a man such as Wade Calhoun.

She worried about it all. She had nothing soft or frilly or—and she blushed mentally—risqué. Something that might make a man look at her like something other than his sister.

Just before camp was made for the night, Polly shrugged. She would have to make do with what she had. There was no other way to go about it that she could see.

Despite his anger, Calhoun had done his job diligently and found a decent spot for the travelers to camp.

Sand hills rolled off to the northeast, but there was grassland northwest across the river, and on their side. There would be decent grazing for the horses and oxen and mules that night. It would be the first time for such a luxury in quite some time.

He tied off the horse, loosened the saddle, and set about gathering firewood and buffalo chips. Though he had done it before, it was not really his job. He was hungry, though. He figured he would get a fire going and have meat cooking by the time the wagons wandered in. That way he wouldn't have to wait too long to eat.

Once the meat was roasting, Calhoun looked over the rifle again. He nodded, having decided what needed to be done.

From one of his saddlebags he pulled some rawhide. He cut a strip about six inches wide and two feet long. He dunked the rawhide into the piddling stripe of water that passed for a creek. Then he wrapped the rawhide as tightly as he could around the rifle's cracked stock. Once that was done, Calhoun propped the rifle up where it would catch the heat from the fire.

He sat back to wait, making an effort to keep his mind blank. He dared not let the thoughts of his past gain control of him again. Thankfully, it was not a long wait before the travelers arrived.

As the wagons creaked into the brushy, wooded campsite, Calhoun directed them into place until Coldhammer took over such work, as was proper.

By then, Calhoun was starving. He hacked off several slices of meat, dropped them onto his tin plate, and wandered off to eat in peace and silence.

The Coldhammers seemed to be about the only ones who ever really appreciated his efforts at preparing food, but Calhoun wanted no company right now.

Polly brought him some coffee and lingered a few moments more than was absolutely necessary.

Calhoun nodded thanks and stared into her deep green eyes for a moment. He thought there was something different about Miss Polly Coldhammer, but he could not be quite sure what it was.

Soon after, Coldhammer himself drifted over. He squatted, ill at ease, as he always was in Calhoun's presence. Coldhammer sipped from his coffee cup. He never had gotten around to speaking to Calhoun about the violence that the guide seemed to invite.

He knew he should have; still should. But he could not bring himself to do it.

Coldhammer finally cleared his throat. "After all the excitement of earlier," he began lamely, "the folks were thinkin' to relax with a little music and dancin'. Would you figure that'd be all right?"

Calhoun could seen no harm in it. If there were Indians about, these damnfool people would not know about it anyway. Besides, he was fairly certain the Sioux would not attack at night. Most tribes didn't, from what he had learned.

"Have at it," he said quietly.

Coldhammer smiled a little as he stood. He had expected to get a hard time from Calhoun. "Thank you, Mister Calhoun," he said. He paused, then asked, "Will you be joinin' us for the festivities?"

"Reckon not."

Coldhammer understood. He nodded, even though Calhoun was no longer looking at him, and he strolled away.

A few minutes later, a guitar, violin, harmonica, and concertina sent their wavering notes drifting up into the gathering night with the smoke of the cook-fires.

The impromptu band was playing "Primrose Lass." The traditional tune swept Calhoun back to his old boyhood home in Tennessee. He had enjoyed it there among the cool, well-watered hollows dappled from the sunlight filtering through the thick stands of oak and ash and hickory. There was a fresh, alive scent about the place that he could remember even now, across all the miles and time.

He rolled a cigarette, trying to push the sights of Tennessee and his boyhood memories out of his mind. He had been gone from Tennessee a long time. He would not go back. Of that he was certain. And he'd be damned if he would let the past haunt him.

Still, his thin face with its proud prow of hawkish nose, was tight with his effort to restrain the thoughts.

The band soon swung into a spirited version of "Phoenix Quickstep," and Calhoun had to fight the urge to tap his boot to the rollicking, danceable tune.

It did allow him to shed the gloomy thoughts of Tennessee and his sister, Ardeth, and Kansas and Lizbeth and Lottie and . . .

He stamped the cigarette out roughly in the dirt and stretched out in his blankets. He hoped Erline Rae would pay him a visit tonight, but he figured that was unlikely. With the festivities going on, she would be occupied. As one of only two—three, Calhoun corrected himself, thinking of Clair Wright—decent-looking single women along with the wagon train, she would not be allowed to sit out a dance.

Neither would Polly, he was certain. She, however, was still out of bounds for him, he decided. He fell asleep wondering again at the difference he had detected in her.

He was awake in the morning long before everyone else. He enjoyed the solitude and chill of the predawn darkness. He built up the Coldhammers' fire, put last night's pot of coffee on to heat, and quickly fried some bacon. He ate hurriedly, since he wanted no company this morning.

Leaving his mess where it lay, he saddled the skewbald horse and rode out, marking the trail he wanted the others to follow.

Within a week, the wagon train had passed the fork of the North and South Platte rivers, and was moving along the North Platte. Just after hitting the North Platte, they had fended off a raid by Kaw Indians, with the loss of only one mule.

After the earlier Sioux attack, the people were not nearly so frightened. The Kaws were far less imposing than the Sioux, and far fewer in number. They had forted up rapidly, but with a minimum of fuss. Two volleys later, the Kaws raced off across the almost flat plain, carting a dead warrior with them.

Without comment, the wagon train reharnessed the teams and moved on.

A day later, they were camped by Chimney Rock, and Polly Coldhammer decided it was time to approach Wade Calhoun.

She waited under her wagon that night, pretending to sleep and hardly daring to breathe. Finally she was sure that her father, mother, and six siblings were sound asleep. Then she carefully slid out from under the wagon and made her way silently to where she knew Calhoun had put his bedroll.

As she neared the spot, she heard soft sounds. They tugged with a little familiarity at her mind, but she could not place them.

She slowed her pace, fright building in her stomach. Heart in her throat, she crept forward and peered around a sandstone boulder that had been deposited in this strange place some time in the distant, forgotten past.

Suddenly she stopped, shocked and hurt beyond belief.

She stood, crouched, watching in fascination as Calhoun and Erline Rae North sported with quiet, though obviously wild and joyful abandon.

Anger, shame, and desire filled Polly, each fighting to predominate. She wanted to vomit, but at the same time she was flushed and felt a heat rise inside her. It was unlike anything she had ever experienced. She did not know what to do.

Calhoun and Erline Rae finally settled down, sated. Calhoun sat up, rolled and lit a cigarette. He sat there, smoking. He was naked, save for a blanket wrapped around his midsection. His broad, strong back gleamed oddly in the pale moonlight. He talked quietly with Erline Rae, and the woman laughed softly.

Polly turned away and headed back toward her father's wagon. She felt tears staining her cheeks and she wiped at them with an angry hand. She wanted to hate Calhoun for this. She felt that he had betrayed her.

She finally realized, though, that she could not hate him. Not totally. She wanted him too much; wanted him with an aching desire that filled her.

She got no sleep that night as she fought with herself silently.

CHAPTER

* 12 *

Polly glared at Calhoun when she gave him his coffee in the morning.

He looked up at her blandly, like he always did, though she thought she might have detected a question in his eyes. As usual, he said nothing. Polly wanted to scream at him.

Her displeasure at him could not last, though. She fought to retain the anger, not wanting to forgive him, but she could not hold out. Two nights later, she made up her mind to go to him again. It was a night when nearly everyone from the wagon train was tired, and all turned in early.

It had rained heavily the day before, which meant today's travel had been through thick mud. It was grueling on horses and animals. Especially since Calhoun had gotten angry at the travelers' renewed complaints. In response, he had kept them in harness for an awfully long time.

As she waited for everyone to fall asleep, Polly thought she might burst from excitement and tension. She wanted to go to Calhoun while it was still too early for Erline Rae to join him.

Wisely, though, she bided her time, biting her lip in anxiety. She spent some of that time wondering about Erline Rae North. The young woman had something of the look of a trollop about her, Polly decided. Polly did, though, acknowledge that it might be her own cattiness making her see that.

Still, Polly wondered. With a father like Sherman North, Erline Rae could not have had an easy childhood. She probably still had it rough, Polly decided. Sympathy for Erline Rae North welled up in Polly's bosom, which made Polly angry. She did not want to have any kind feelings for a woman she now considered the utmost in competition for Wade Calhoun.

As soon as she thought it was safe, Polly crawled out of the wagon. The Coldhammer family, like most of the others, was sleeping inside tonight lest they get rained on some more. She gingerly made her way toward where Calhoun was camped.

She was relieved to find that Calhoun was alone under the small canvas lean-to he had put up over his bedroll.

She whispered his name, hoping that he was still awake.

"Miss Polly?" he asked. For one of the few times in his life, he heard surprise in his own voice.

"Yes." Her voice cracked because of her dry throat. She walked up tentatively. Feeling a touch of fear bite into her bowels, she sat on the edge of the blankets. She looked like a deer ready to bolt.

"What're you doin' here?" Calhoun asked. He was wary. Young women like Polly Coldhammer did not come to the bed of a man like Wade Calhoun in the middle of the night, as a rule.

Polly was speechless. But she hoped that her

eyes and the way she held herself would explain things, if only a little.

Apparently they did, even in the darkness of the overcast night. Only the dully glowing embers of a small fire Calhoun had made near his shelter spread any light at all. It apparently was enough, though, since Calhoun moved toward her with a grace Polly had never expected in so rough and violent a man.

Calhoun kissed her softly.

Polly was too frightened to respond, but when Calhoun leaned back, she smiled weakly and hung her head. "Wasn't much help, was I?" she asked.

Calhoun shrugged. He knew now why she was there. Her actions had confirmed that for him. They also loudly proclaimed her lack of experience.

He was in no hurry to push her along, especially since he still wondered why someone like Polly would come to him like this. He figured her innocence precluded any dastardly ulterior motive. On the other hand, he found it hard to believe that she was here simply because she could not resist him. He was not vain enough to think that all women desired him.

They chatted quietly for a little while. Actually, it was Polly who did most of the talking. Soon enough, and Polly found herself relaxing. Before long, she realized she had moved closer to him and eventually she was resting her head on Calhoun's chest, where it joined the shoulder. She felt his arms around her. And then she realized she was ready for him. Polly tilted her head back, awaiting his kiss.

It was not long in coming.

* * *

Within another week, they were nearing Fort Laramie. Polly had visited Calhoun at night several times, as had Erline Rae. He gave no thought to worrying about having the two of them as lovers. He figured life would be easier if the two did not know about each other, but if they found out, he would deal with it.

Not knowing that Polly already knew about Erline Rae, he worried more about her finding out than vice versa. He figured Erline Rae had been around enough that she would accept such a thing as normal. He was certain that Polly would not be able to handle it, though.

"You aimin' to stop at the fort, Mister Calhoun?" Coldhammer asked, riding up alongside the guide.

Smoke from the fort's fires hung in the air, visible to the travelers.

Calhoun shrugged.

Coldhammer was growing weary of Calhoun's uncommunicativeness. Though there was little he could do about it, he didn't have to like it any. At times like these, he figured he would be happy to be rid of the untalkative, surly guide.

"The animals as well as folks could use some rest," Coldhammer said. "A few of the wagons need repairs, and there's some folks could do with extra supplies."

Calhoun nodded. "We'll stop."

He pulled up and sat with wrists crossed on the saddlehorn, reins held loosely in his hands. "Y'all do know that the worst is to come, don't you, Mister Coldhammer?"

The wagon master looked at him in surprise. "How's it worse?" he asked, trying to mask his discomfit.

"We've been travelin' the flats since we left Saint Joe. Not much farther on, we'll hit some mean-ass mountains. It'll take all you got in you to get through 'em."

Coldhammer nodded. "All the more reason to take a few days to rest up. Make sure the animals are in the best health we can expect. Be certain our gear will stand up to the demands."

Calhoun nodded and jiggled the reins. They moved on.

They stayed near the fort for several days, making repairs to wagons, enjoying the hospitality of the soldiers, and even gawking at some of the Indians who were camped nearby.

Calhoun took no part in the latter. They were mostly Sioux around here, and he hated the Sioux with all his heart. They might appear to be tame Indians here in the shadow of the fort, but Calhoun knew better. It was all he could do to keep from attacking some of the peaceful Indians who loitered around the fort.

So he kept to himself, which was usual anyway. He spent a little of his hundred and some dollars on personal supplies he might need—powder, ball, percussion caps, some food supplies.

Rollie Pepperdine had about fully recovered from the whupping Calhoun had administered, but he had himself checked over by the post surgeon. The doctor declared him fit.

Pepperdine was still embarrassed about the beating, so he moved humbly around the fort and wagons, as he had since it had happened.

His cronies, though, managed to convince him soon enough that he had nothing to be ashamed of. After all, Calhoun had taken unfair advantage of him, hitting him when he wasn't looking, belting him with a rifle butt. Anyone would have been at a disadvantage after such treatment.

It did not take long for Pepperdine to take such talk to heart. Before the caravan left the fort, Pepperdine had begun swaggering around like in the old days. He even challenged Calhoun to another fight, right in front of the soldiers and travelers.

"No," Calhoun said flatly.

"Afraid?" Pepperdine asked, sneering.

His friends behind him sniggered in derision.

Calhoun felt the anger boil up in him again. But he had not gotten this far in life by letting himself be goaded into things.

"Of you?" Calhoun asked. His voice was thick with scorn. "Shoot, I'd as soon be scared of Charlie Borgum's two-year-old."

Some travelers laughed, and even Billy Quince had to stifle a chuckle.

Pepperdine did not laugh; did not so much as smile. He seethed. "Why you chickenshit little—"

"Watch your mouth, boy," Calhoun snapped. "There's ladies about."

"I'll talk however I damn well please," Pepperdine retorted. "'Less'n you're figurin' to stop me."

"I done it twice," Calhoun said quietly. "I'll not

have trouble doin' it again, should you force my hand."

"Well I *am* forcin' your hand, goddamnit. I—"

"*Mister* Pepperdine!" a voice roared.

Pepperdine slapped his flabby lips shut and looked stupidly around for the source of the sound.

The post commander, Maj. Miles Mangum, stood a little to the side. His fists were on his hips; his face was livid with anger. The wind whipped at his bushy mane of snow-white hair.

"What?" Pepperdine asked. He was surly.

"You have been asked to watch your mouth around these womenfolk. I'd suggest you take that request to heart."

"Or what?" Pepperdine's voice had lost none of its nastiness.

"Or I'll have you thrown into the stockade."

"I ain't no goddamn blue-belly soldier boy," Pepperdine snapped.

"Mister Pepperdine," Mangum said with a sigh. He sounded as if he were addressing a child rather than a hulking brute. "I must confess that I have noted you are not a soldier. Were you, I would've had you shot a long time ago. I still might."

He paused, looking sternly at a suddenly uncomfortable Rollie Pepperdine. "I am military commander for this district. That means I hold sway over everyone and everything that passes through the territory."

Once more he paused. It was silent on the parade grounds, as people waited for the fort commander to continue.

"Now, Mister Pepperdine, if I tell my troops to throw you in the stockade, do you think they'd refuse because you're a civilian? Do you?"

"No," Pepperdine mumbled. He was angry and discomfited. This was the second time in as many weeks that Calhoun had embarrassed him in front of the others. He vowed that it would not happen again.

"Since that's settled, suppose you and your friends just mosey on."

"But I challenged that son of a . . . him," Pepperdine said defiantly. He pointed a stubby finger at Calhoun.

Mangum turned patiently toward Calhoun. "Did you accept his challenge, Mister Calhoun?" he asked.

"Nope."

"That's 'cause he's a chickensh . . . he's a coward," Pepperdine bellowed in indignation.

"I believe you have the wrong man here, Mister Pepperdine," Mangum said. His voice was deceptively quiet. "I have known Mister Calhoun for some years. I have ridden with him, fought at his side. He is no coward, sir."

"Then why the hell . . . why won't he fight me, then?"

"As I understand it, he has already shown he can take you in a fight."

Pepperdine flushed angrily at the sound of laughter directed at him. "He took unfair advantage. Hit me with his da . . . his rifle."

"Broke the rifle," Calhoun said. Almost a smile touched his lips.

Mangum rubbed a brawny hand over the lower half of his face, trying to hide his smile. "Sounds like it was a fair fight to me, Mister Pepperdine," Mangum allowed.

"Like he . . ." Pepperdine clamped his mouth shut, trying to form a retort that did not include any profanity. "It weren't no fair fight," he finally snapped. "I want a fair fight."

"Mister Calhoun?" Mangum queried, looking at his old scout.

"As long as it's between him and me, it ain't gonna be a fair fight," Calhoun said. Once again something that almost resembled a smile flickered across his face. He watched Pepperdine a few moments before turning away.

It took Pepperdine a little while to get the implication of Calhoun's words, and to realize he had been insulted. His eyes bulged as he looked at Calhoun's back. "Come back here and fight, you Injun-lovin' son of a . . ."

Calhoun spun back to face Pepperdine. He had one of his Dragoons in his hand, cocked and ready.

Pepperdine gulped, knowing he was looking at death.

Calhoun walked slowly toward Pepperdine, the pistol out. At five yards, he stopped, lowered the revolver a little, and fired. The bullet tore a hole in the inside thigh of Pepperdine's trousers, about midway up.

Pepperdine swallowed hard. He knew he was in trouble now. He ached to go for his gun, but he knew he would die for certain in such a case. If he just stood still, he might live.

Calhoun fired three more times. Each pistol ball crawled a little closer to Calhoun's privates. The last bullet punched a hole in the baggy crotch of Pepperdine's pants.

Pepperdine lost control of his internal functions, and he soiled himself.

Calhoun moseyed up to Pepperdine and lightly placed the muzzle of his Dragoon under Pepperdine's nose. He tried not to breathe, hoping he would not have to smell the big man.

"If you ever say such words to me again," Calhoun said tightly, "I'll splatter what little brains you got all over. Understand?"

"Yes," Pepperdine squeaked.

Calhoun pulled the pistol away and eased the hammer down. He turned and began walking away. As he did, he slid the Dragoon away. He had no fear, since he knew Major Mangum and his troops would not allow Pepperdine or his friends to back shoot him.

CHAPTER

✴ 13 ✴

The wagon train pulled out the next morning. No one had seen Pepperdine since his altercation with Calhoun the afternoon before, but he could be heard snapping and snarling from inside his wagon for most of the night. He sounded drunk.

Two nights after they left Fort Laramie, Coldhammer decided that another dance would be in order. He hoped the festivities would take the travelers' minds off the renewed harshness of their trek after the few days of enjoying the relative comforts of the fort.

Though he would never admit it to anyone, Coldhammer also harbored a hope that such a celebration might ease the tensions that were rapidly building up again between Wade Calhoun and the five men with whom Rollie Pepperdine associated.

Calhoun sat with his back against a rock, several yards from the wagons. He wanted to disassociate himself from the goings-on as much as possible, since he had little interest in the activities. He did not dance and he was not much of a man for fraternizing.

Later, after the instruments had been put away

and the people had gone to bed, Calhoun lay in his blankets, waiting. Before long, Polly arrived.

Calhoun and Polly were engaged in pleasurable pursuits when Erline Rae ambled up. She stopped, looking down at Calhoun and Polly. Utter surprise was stamped on her creamy, olive face.

She had not come to see Calhoun since just before the wagon train had gotten to Fort Laramie. Calhoun had wondered why, but he was not really concerned about it. He held no claim on her; nor she on him.

Besides, he figured that she had not come around to visit simply because there were too many people around the fort.

In the two days since, he was pretty sure that she had been kept occupied by others. The thought annoyed him. Not so much because she was most likely with another man; that meant nothing to him. What bothered him was that she was being forced into such things—by her father no less.

To Wade Calhoun, a man like Sherman North should be gut shot and left to die slowly.

"What's goin' on here?" Erline Rae puffed. Her face was flushed with anger and shock.

"I expect you can figure that out," Calhoun said evenly. He sat up, partially blocking Polly from Erline Rae's view.

"How could you sport with that . . . trollop when I'm right here?" Erline Rae demanded. Her voice was withering in its disdain and rising in volume.

Calhoun shrugged. He figured what he did was his business. He owed Erline Rae nothing.

"Don't you just sit there lookin' like you don't give a hoot about me, you double-dealin'—"

"Best lower your voice," Calhoun warned.

"Why? So the others don't find out what you're doin' here with that little witch?" Erline Rae's voice was cold. Her body was rigid with anger as she stood with arms crossed over her chest.

"You'll be the one come out lookin' the worse for all this," Calhoun said rationally.

Erline Rae realized with dread that Calhoun was right. Making it worse was the sudden knowledge that it was too late now. She could hear other people stumbling in their direction.

She turned, frightened, to see if her father was among them; praying that he was not. Was he to figure something was going on here, his retribution would not be pleasant.

Calhoun turned in his bedroll and said quietly but urgently, "Get your duds and go."

Polly looked blank for a minute.

"Go on off in the dark somewhere and dress. Come back out here from another way like nothin's happened. Your pa asks, tell him you had to answer nature's call when you heard the commotion."

He sighed. He probably hadn't spoken that much at one time since he was twelve.

"But what about her?" Polly asked, pointing to Erline Rae.

"She ain't gonna say nothin'. Go."

Polly grabbed her garments, jumped up, and fled.

"What the hell's going on here?" Sherman North demanded. He strode up, trying to look self-important.

Bass Cutler waddled up alongside him, as did Tiny Bates.

"I asked you all what was goin' on here," North demanded again, his voice rising.

Calhoun looked at Erline Rae and then back to North and his two companions. Calhoun glared at the three. He had had no trouble with any of the men since he had beaten the stuffing out of Rollie Pepperdine. He suspected that peace might be about to end.

"Erline Rae?" North asked, voice hardening. He looked at his daughter, anger stamped on his face.

"Nothin's goin' on here, Pa," she said. Her voice quavered with fright. "Honest." Though she was still worried, she was beginning to regain control of herself.

"Then what're you doin' here standin' 'round in such a mussed state? And with Calhoun sittin' over there wearin' little more than a dumb look?"

"I had to tend to personal business, Pa," Erline Rae said. She looked properly embarrassed at mentioning such things in mixed company. "I was goin' out yonder a little when I tripped over Mister Calhoun. I let out a yell . . ." She tapered off but came back strong.

"I fell and hollered again. When Mister Calhoun started gettin' up to see if was I all right, it startled me all the more. I was thinkin' those Indians had come on back and all, and I just started yellin' . . ."

She finally paused, figuring she had said enough.

Calhoun almost grinned. He was generally a humorless man, but he was mightily impressed with the performance Erline Rae had just made. He had not seen the likes of it since he had stopped by that fancy theater hall in New Orleans a few years back. She had seemed to have mixed the proper amount of surprise, embarrassment, and defensiveness.

North seemed far less impressed and far more skeptical. He eyed his daughter warily. Then he glanced at Calhoun, who stared evenly back at him.

Finally North grunted. He was unconvinced, but he didn't think there was much he could do for now. Not with all these people around. Was he to berate his daughter in public, he would bring both of them into disrepute. He was loath to do that, since he prided himself on keeping his private life under wraps. It was a wise way to be for a man like him, considering how disreputable his private life was.

"Come," North ordered. He whirled and walked brusquely away.

"Let's all hit the hay," Coldhammer called out.

When no one showed any signs of moving, he said forcefully, "Come on, folks, move on. There's nothin' to be standin' around here for. We had us a long day today and I expect tomorrow will bring more of the same. So, back to your shut-eye."

The people began drifting off.

Calhoun watched as Coldhammer gave his daughter a questioning look before heading to his wagon with Polly and the other members of his family.

Calhoun took a deep breath and let it out. At the same time, he eased down the hammer of the Colt Dragoon he was holding under the blanket partially wrapped around him.

After a few moments, he turned in and went to sleep. It was a long time in coming, though, considering his state of arousal, and the problems he could foresee for himself.

He was almost amused when he thought, *Well, at least it ain't a horse causin' the troubles this time.*

Calhoun rode out the next morning ahead of the wagons, like usual. As he did occasionally, he brought two mules with him. He had a hankering for fresh buffalo meat and hoped to find a herd during his travels.

He had been up and gone before the others had even woken. That bothered him a little, since North and some of the others would think he was trying to avoid them.

He finally put such thoughts behind him. They were getting him nowhere, and he did not think them worthy of his time. Not with all the annoyance they caused in him.

Sometime late in the morning, he skirted a stalled wagon train. There were maybe thirty wagons in all. Calhoun pulled up on a ridge and sat for a few minutes, watching silently.

The campsite was full of activity, not much of it pleasant for those people that Calhoun could see. Several men were working to jack up a wagon that listed far over on its side with a broken rear wheel. Two men were butchering a cow.

Other men were hauling furniture and other belongings out of wagons. They tossed the goods to the side of the trail. A number of women stood tight-lipped or crying nearby, seeing much of their lives cast by the wayside. That fact was just another insult in the harsh life they had encountered since they had left their homes.

Many of the other people were gathered around a freshly dug grave. It was a small grave, and Calhoun figured it was for a child. The wailing of the bereaved could be heard even up on the ridge.

Calhoun shook his head. There was nothing he could do here. He and the Coldhammer wagon train passed graves by the dozens every day, it seemed. He had seen more than his share of them, too, long before he signed on with Barrett Coldhammer.

As he rode on, heading westward, he calculated that Coldhammer's wagon train would pass this one within a couple of hours. He stopped a moment, rubbing his hard jaw as he thought.

Then he nodded. He swung the horse eastward and rode swiftly for a mile or so.

He marked the trail well, wanting Coldhammer and the others to give this stalled wagon train a wide berth. Coldhammer's people had enough of their own troubles. They did not need to be subjected to the misfortunes of these unlucky pilgrims.

Calhoun moved on, slowly, heading mostly westward once again.

He passed several possible campsites, but did not stop. He figured they were not far enough along on the trail.

Along about midafternoon, though, he found a decent spot. He followed his back trail and then returned to the campsite, marking the trail as he rode. He turned north. A little earlier, he had seen a few buffalo less than two miles away.

When he returned to the campsite, both mules were heavily laden with rich, bloody buffalo meat.

CHAPTER

* 14 *

Calhoun spent that night alone, but the next night, Erline Rae was back. The dark young woman made no apologies nor gave any explanations. She simply appeared at Calhoun's bedroll, shucked her simple garments, and slid in beside him.

She also made love with a wildness and fury she had not exhibited earlier. That surprised Calhoun, but only a little.

When she was ready to leave in the morning, it was dangerously close to dawn. Erline Rae knelt and kissed Calhoun one last time.

"Maybe now you'll forget that little girl, eh?" she whispered. Then she hurried away.

A few minutes later, Calhoun rose, yawned, and stretched lazily. He pulled on his clothes and hung his gun belt around his waist. He was tired, having gotten too little sleep. Otherwise, he felt pretty good.

He finally headed toward the Coldhammer fire and settled in quietly.

As Polly handed him a plate of bacon and biscuits, he asked in a low voice, "Everything all right?"

The golden-haired young woman looked at him blankly, not understanding.

"The other night . . ." he hinted. He had not yet

had a chance to question her about the night they had almost been caught together. It appeared that no one was the wiser, since Coldhammer had acted no differently toward him than before.

"Oh, yes," Polly whispered, as realization struck. "I'm just fine." Her eyes gleamed in the knowledge of the secret she shared with Calhoun. "Neither Pa nor Ma suspect anything."

She hesitated an instant, then added, "Thank you." Polly blushed, grateful for Calhoun's quick thinking. She would have been ruined had people found out what she was doing that night.

Calhoun nodded and silently ate his meal.

He was just finishing his coffee when he heard an angry shout. He turned just in time to see Sherman North haul off and smack his daughter in the face, knocking her down.

Erline Rae had gotten up, and North whacked her again, knocking her down once more.

Tiny Bates giggled in that high-pitched, deranged voice of his. He took two mincing steps forward and kicked Erline Rae.

The young woman said nothing, but even across the camp Calhoun could tell that she was in pain.

North bent and began slapping and punching his daughter with grim determination.

"Shit," Calhoun growled quietly in annoyance. He dropped his plate.

He was pushing himself up when Coldhammer and two other men charged across the camp. Calhoun followed more slowly and stopped a little distance away.

Coldhammer grabbed North by the back of the neck and hauled him up, away from Erline Rae.

Coldhammer was not the bravest man in the world, but he had fought in the Mexican War. He usually could be counted on to do what was necessary. He was nearly livid with rage at the sight of North beating a young woman. His daughter, no less.

"You'll leave your hands off that girl, Mister North. Or I'll take the lash to you myself," Coldhammer growled.

"Get away from me, damn your hide," North snapped. He jerked and twisted, trying to get away from Coldhammer's strong grip. He had no success and finally gave up the struggle.

"Erline's my daughter, and I'll treat her any goddamn way I choose," he screeched, words cutting out angrily.

"Not as long as you're with my wagon train you won't," Coldhammer said steadily.

"How're you gonna stop me?" North asked with a sneer.

Nearby, Bates giggled.

"I'll put you in irons if I have to." Coldhammer let the man go. "Now, I don't cotton to a man beatin' a woman, 'specially his own flesh and blood. I don't know just what's got into you, but I want it to stop."

"Damnit, all this is his fault," North said, pointing around Coldhammer. His voice had turned both defensive and whiny.

"Whose?" the wagon master asked, turning.

"Calhoun's," North said adamantly.

Calhoun moseyed a little closer.

"What's he had to do with it?" Coldhammer asked, facing North again.

"He despoiled my Erline," North roared. He flapped his mouth shut, suddenly looking embarrassed. He knew he had said too much.

Sherman North was not a man much given to thought. He was angrier than he ever had been, ever since this morning. He had woken early and gone off to make water. He had spotted Erline Rae just coming back to the wagon. He could tell from her look what she had been up to.

It had made him snap. It was not so much that he was all that protective of his daughter's virtue. Not with what he had called upon her to do. He just saw it as another man—Calhoun—usurping his powers and taking something that North felt he owned, and doing so without paying for it. So he had opened his mouth without thinking.

Now he tried to cover his mistake with a stern visage.

"Is that true, Mister Calhoun?" Coldhammer asked, looking over his shoulder.

"That's none of your concern, Mister Coldhammer," Calhoun said evenly. He knew half the people wouldn't believe him if he denied it. He could expose North's treatment of Erline Rae. Doing that, however, would be to put Erline Rae in a poor light with the others. He saw no reason to do that.

"I believe it is," Coldhammer said, his voice hardening a little. He began to feel he had let things go too far. He knew he should have stopped all this a long time ago. He was as much to blame as either of these two.

"Don't matter what you believe."

Coldhammer thought about that for a little while. It was, he decided, true. Whether Calhoun had had his way with Erline Rae or not concerned only the guide, the girl, and her father. Maybe God, too. It certainly did not give North an excuse to pound the bejesus out of his daughter, or anyone else.

Seeing the wagon master's doubting look, North shouted, "I demand you do somethin' about Calhoun, Coldhammer."

"You keep your hands off your daughter, North," Coldhammer said icily. "You hear me?"

Coldhammer did not wait for an answer. He spun on his boot heel and strode away. He was furious. Part of that was anger at himself for having let things get out of hand. He wasn't sure what to do about all this now. It was most likely too late to really do much anyway.

He had not gotten far when he heard a shout and snarl behind him. He jerked his head around, just in time to see North run into Calhoun's hard right fist.

"Damnit to hell and back," Coldhammer snapped under his breath. He spun around and ran toward the two new combatants.

Erline Rae stepped in his path, before the wagon master could get to Calhoun and North.

"Don't," she said quietly but forcefully.

"But, ma'am—"

"No, Mister Coldhammer," Erline Rae insisted. "He's had this comin' for years."

"But he's your pa."

"Only because he had his way with some woman unfortunate enough to smile at him once." There was bitterness in the words, but no anger. She could not change her life; or at least not her past.

Coldhammer was not happy about it, but he could understand. He had met people like her before; people who had no control over the way their lives had started. He nodded, and watched the fight.

Calhoun had decked North straight off, when North had run into his fist. He could have finished North off then and there, but he decided maybe Erline Rae would not like that. So he thought he would give North another chance to call it quits.

North pulled himself up slowly. He had the sudden notion that he had taken on a chore far bigger than he was able to handle. To look at Calhoun, one would never know he had so much iron in his fists.

North shook his head and wriggled his jaw several times. Everything seemed to be working right, though it was painful.

"Best give it a rest, old man," Calhoun warned. He had gotten up not long ago, feeling as good as he ever did. North had quickly spoiled what had been a fine day. He was of no mood to stand here and fool around with some demented oaf who seemed bent on self-destruction.

North still stood there, trying to collect his withering wits.

Calhoun watched him, still trying to stay aware of everyone else. It was impossible, but he at least knew no one was pulling a gun on him. He also suspected that Coldhammer would try to make sure that no guns were drawn.

Suddenly, Tiny Bates was on Calhoun's back. The maniacal little man whooped crazily and he wrapped one scrawny arm around Calhoun's throat. With his other hand, he punched Calhoun repeatedly.

"Goddamn fool," Calhoun snapped. He reached back over his shoulder with his left hand and grabbed a hunk of Bates's shirt. He ducked forward and yanked at the same time.

Bates came sailing over Calhoun's shoulder. Calhoun let go of the little man's shirt. Bates bounced and yelped in shocked surprise.

Before Bates stopped rolling, Calhoun stepped quickly up to him and stomped on Bates's stomach twice with his boot heel.

"Don't ever pull a damnfool . . ." Calhoun started. He stopped and smashed his right fist backhanded into North's face.

North had used the opportunity—or so he saw it —of Calhoun's preoccupation with Bates to edge up. When he thought Calhoun's attention entirely on Bates, North pounced.

Calhoun had been aware of North the whole time. He wasn't sure the older man would really try anything, but he was prepared just in case.

What he wasn't prepared for was Bass Cutler's immense obesity.

Cutler slammed into his side, throwing all this three hundred-plus pounds into the wheezing effort.

Calhoun went tumbling sideways, swearing quietly. Anger flashed through him at having been taken by surprise.

The anger boiled up and out as Calhoun stopped rolling. He caught a glimpse of North and Cutler heading for him. He almost smiled. He could easily kill both men now. One smooth move up onto a knee, a Colt Dragoon in his hand. The two wouldn't even know what hit them.

That, however, would be too easy, he figured. It also might get him killed. Coldhammer was a reasonable man, but shooting Cutler and North like this would be considered cold-blooded murder. He supposed he could kill Coldhammer easily enough, but he saw no need for that.

Nor for killing the two coming at him. Not when his fists and strength would suffice.

Calhoun surged up to his feet and moved toward the two men, who were still charging at him.

He shifted toward his side a little and lowered his shoulder. The hard edge of his shoulder jammed into Cutler's breastbone with numbing force.

Cutler, who always had trouble breathing normally because of his ponderous weight, choked and gasped. Involuntarily, he bent. He sputtered and turned ashen as he tried to draw a breath around the pain and his flab.

Calhoun spun half to the side. He locked his fists together and swung them up. Then they descended with tremendous force, landing on the back of Cutler's fat neck. Cutler buckled and fell flat on his face in the dirt.

North had stumbled to a halt a few feet away, sep-

arated from Calhoun by Cutler's bulk. He looked at
Calhoun, fright coloring his eyes. His right hand
twitched, heading toward his belt, where he usually
carried his Colt revolver.

He realized with a shock that the pistol had fallen
out when Calhoun had backhanded him.

Calhoun grinned viciously.

"You're lucky I ain't got my sidearm," North
snapped, trying to cover up his fear with bravado.

"No," Calhoun said mildly, "you're the lucky one."

North looked at him blankly, too stupid to understand that if he had had a pistol on him, he would
have died.

Calhoun stepped over Cutler, moving toward
North. Out of the corner of his left eye, he caught
sight of Rollie Pepperdine heading toward him. He
figured he would have to lambaste North quickly,
and then turn to face the large, brutish Pepperdine.

Then Coldhammer had moved forward. His Rem-
ington pistol was in his hand, pointed at Pepperdine's large torso.

"This ain't your affair, Mister Pepperdine," Coldhammer said. "This is between Mister Calhoun and
Mister North."

Pepperdine growled angrily but stopped.

Calhoun grinned wickedly at North again.

North looked sick. He wanted to run, but there
was nowhere to go. The growing ring of people surrounding him and Calhoun would have made running foolhardy anyway.

He leaped at Calhoun. He found only air, though,
as Calhoun had moved to the side. He realized with

a sour feeling in his stomach that he was in serious trouble. He grunted as one of Calhoun's hard fists cracked into his cheekbone.

North fell, hoping that if he was down, Calhoun would not bother him any longer.

Calhoun, however, was not feeling that magnanimous. He reached down and grabbed North's shirt and hauled him half up off the ground.

"You like whuppin' folks while they're down," Calhoun snarled. "Let's see how you like it from the other side."

Calhoun pounded hard punches into North's stomach, chest, and face. Not enough to do any real, permanent damage, but enough that North would be sore for days.

Calhoun also hoped it would make North reconsider the next time he had the urge to whale the tar out of Erline Rae.

Finally Calhoun stopped. He let go of North's shirt. North fell. Calhoun surveyed the damage he had wrought, decided it wasn't as bad as it could be, and calmly walked back toward Coldhammer's fire.

CHAPTER
* 15 *

Calhoun rode out soon after, taking up his position far ahead of the wagons, as he always did.

Before leaving, he had taken enough time for another cup of coffee and a cigarette. He had saddled his horse and struck his little camp slowly. It was as if he were defying anyone to challenge him.

He had left without thanking Coldhammer for stepping in. He hadn't really needed the help. Still, Coldhammer did not have to place himself in jeopardy like that, and Calhoun appreciated the gesture.

Calhoun had wanted to thank Coldhammer, but such was not his way. He had considered doing so when Coldhammer had come up and nervously recommended that he speed his movements and get out on the trail.

The suggestion angered him. He knew Coldhammer was just watching out for the welfare of the wagon train, but Calhoun always got his hackles up when people started telling him what to do.

In response, he had slowed even more, having that extra cup of coffee. Finally, though, he was ready to get moving. There was no good reason for hanging around any longer anyway. He mounted up and rode out of camp.

As he rode, he thought about Coldhammer, and North, and the others. He knew there would be more trouble with the six men traveling together in the two big wagons. He wondered what they were even doing out here, traveling with Coldhammer's wagon train.

Such thoughts were getting him nowhere, though. He had no answers to any of the questions. So instead, he thought about Polly and Erline Rae. There, too, was a vexatious problem, and he wondered where it would lead. He did not want to hurt either woman, nor see them hurt by others.

While he had no permanent designs on either of them, he liked both. Even if he could not restore his former intimate relationships with both, he wanted at least to regain their friendship.

Calhoun especially worried about Erline Rae. She was liable to face a real hard time of things now that he had beaten her father so badly. He had to be out on the trail most, if not all the day, which meant she might be at her father's mercy.

Calhoun only hoped that the beating he had given North would dissuade North from attacking his daughter, at least for a while. He also suspected that Coldhammer would watch over the young woman.

All those thoughts became unimportant along about midday, however. That's when he spotted a small war party of Arapahos less than a mile across the plains to the south.

He edged closer to the Arapahos, wanting to see

if there were others about. He wanted to head off another confrontation between the wagon train and some Indians, if he could help it.

While these five were not enough to attack the travelers, he was concerned that there might be others nearby. It was not inconceivable that around here there might be a camp near enough to gain sufficient reinforcements.

"Damn," he cursed. The five warriors had spotted him.

They howled and set out after Calhoun, maybe a half mile away. He patted his horse on the neck and said, "Reckon we're about to see what you're made of, old boy."

He reined his horse around and galloped off, heading north. The Arapahos were in hot pursuit.

Soon after, Calhoun reached the North Platte River. He followed its meandering course roughly westward, whipping his horse hard. He passed several possible campsites but didn't feel right about any of them. Not with the Arapahos so close behind.

He finally found one he thought would serve. He jerked the horse to a halt and tumbled off the animal. While the horse slurped water from the river, Calhoun scribbled a hasty note. He jammed the crinkly paper into the fork of a small tree and marked the tree. He hoped Coldhammer would be able to spot it.

Then Calhoun was back on the horse and racing along the riverbank again. He wanted to keep the Arapahos away from the campsite, if he could. He also wanted to find a decent place to cross the river.

He glanced back frequently, trying to keep tabs on the Indians. As he galloped out of the campsite, the warriors were less than a quarter mile behind. Such nearness encouraged them, and they quirted their ponies hard.

Calhoun was a little surprised at the performance of his skewbald horse. With his luck with horses, he expected the animal to break a leg the first mile. The horse showed no signs of weakening, though.

Calhoun finally saw what looked like a good spot to ford the river. He eased the horse down into the shallow, muddy water. The river was not deep but it seemed a mile wide.

Calhoun moved the horse across as quickly as he could, which wasn't too fast. While there might not be as much quicksand here as back in the sand hill area, it was a possibility. He had to be careful not to get caught.

He was about halfway across when the Arapahos arrived. The warriors screeched at him, shaking their fists and taunting him. One fired several arrows at him.

Calhoun had taken one look behind him when he first heard the Indians arrive. Then he turned his face forward again. He could not worry about the arrows. He knew an arrow could be fatal at well over a hundred yards, and he was closer than that. Still, worrying about it would do him no good. He just rode on.

A minute later, he felt a sharp stinging pain in his leg. He looked down to see an arrow sticking out of his left calf. He could feel blood dripping down into his boot already.

"Shit," he muttered. "Goddamn Indians."

He snatched his rifle out of the scabbard. Stopping the horse, he swung around in the saddle. He took quick aim and fired.

An Arapaho fell out of his saddle, landing with a splash in the water.

"How do you like them apples," Calhoun snapped as he slid the rifle away. He spurred his horse on.

He stopped on the southern bank of the river and turned his horse sideways. He watched the warriors struggling across the river. He nodded. He reached down, grabbed the shaft of the arrow, and jerked it.

The arrow point tore his flesh and muscle, but it came out. Calhoun held it out to arm's length in the direction of the warriors. Then he threw it into the river and spit after it.

The race began anew. After another mile, Calhoun began to worry about the horse. The animal had been running steadily for more than an hour. It was bound to run down sooner or later.

A few miles farther on, he entered the Rattlesnake Hills. The Arapahos were still fairly close on him, though he had widened the gap a little. He slowed the horse a bit, and within minutes, a bit more.

The Rattlesnake Hills had a few decent-size peaks, but they were not mountains. They were thickly forested in spots, though, and had their share of cliffs and sharp, deep canyons.

Calhoun led the four remaining warriors on a merry chase through the hills, across some plains and ridges, and then circled back into the hills again.

After a while, he decided his horse needed a rest, so Calhoun pulled up. He loosened the saddle and let the animal breathe. He quickly reloaded his rifle and perched behind some rocks, watching his back trail.

The Arapahos eventually appeared again. They were moving in fits and starts. Calhoun smiled grimly. The Arapahos might be good at following a trail, but he was pretty good at hiding one. It was especially easy in the thick grass of the rocky Rattlesnake Hills. It took the Indians some effort to be able to follow him.

Calhoun rested the rifle along the top of the rock and waited some more. He wanted the warriors within decent rifle distance, but he didn't want them getting too close to him either.

After perhaps half an hour, the Arapahos, moving in single file up a narrow trail with a cliff on one side, came into sight about three hundred yards off.

Calhoun stood. Leaving the rifle where it was, he walked back and tightened his saddle. He strolled to the rock. The warriors were a little more than two hundred fifty yards off. He fired.

The leading Arapaho fell, dead before he hit. The second warrior's pony almost trampled on the body. That warrior did manage to get the horse to dance around his companion's corpse.

Calhoun reloaded unhurriedly. Then he rose. He stood defiantly for a moment, then turned and headed for his horse. He rode off.

Moments later, the Arapahos followed, and the chase was on again.

Calhoun finally lost the Indians. Or maybe they just grew tired of chasing him after he had shot down that second warrior. Whatever, the Arapahos peeled off, and he was alone again.

Since it was nearly dark, he found a decent spot where he thought he would be relatively safe. He pulled to a stop and surveyed the area.

There was a shallow cave gouged into the stony side of a hill. A small splash of water ran down the rocks and pooled a few feet from the cave. There was plenty of wood in the heavily treed spot.

He took good care of the horse, rubbing the animal down as best he could with a brush and then some sweet grass. He wished he had some grain for the horse; the animal deserved it. He didn't, though, and the skewbald would have to make do with forage. Fortunately, there was plenty of grass.

After caring for the horse, he gathered firewood and started a small fire. It was just about full dark now. He wanted to look at the wound in his leg. To do that, he would need light. He also would need food. He had not eaten since gnawing down a few strips of buffalo jerky around noon, just before finding the Arapahos.

Calhoun generally rode prepared. This was no exception. He had a small coffeepot, which he filled with water. Adding coffee, he set it on the fire. Then he shredded some salted buffalo into a pot. He added a potato and some water. That, too, went on the fire.

While he waited for the food, he looked at his wounded leg. He cut the pants a little and washed away the blood. The wound was not as bad as he had feared. He tied his dirty bandanna around it after it was cleaned.

Then he ate and turned in.

In the morning, Calhoun headed toward the river, moving southwesterly to bisect it farther west than where he had crossed it yesterday. Along the way, he kept his eyes open for any sign of Arapahos, but he found none.

At the North Platte, he stopped and checked his leg again. It was tender but not very much. He did not figure the wound would hamper him.

He crossed the river, but only long enough to mark the trail. It was as good a place for the wagons to ford the river as any. He also left a note for Cold-hammer, telling the wagon master he was all right and would meet up with the wagon train at day's end. He did not explain what had happened.

Calhoun waded the shallow river back to the north bank and turned west, following the river fairly closely. Soon after, he passed Independence Rock. He did not even consider this as a possible campsite since it was so abused. Indeed, it looked like a wagon train had been there the night before.

That bothered him a little, since with a good day, Coldhammer's wagon train might overtake this one, but not with enough time to put it too far behind. He shrugged. There was nothing he could do about it.

Soon after, he was through the Devil's Gate. Just beyond it, he saw a wagon train stopped. He assumed it was the one that had camped at Independence Rock last night. It looked as if several of the wagons were broken down.

Calhoun did not really gloat, but he felt relieved. With a good push, Coldhammer's people ought to be able to put some distance between themselves and this group.

He rode back a mile or two and wrote another note to Coldhammer, telling him about the other wagon train, and urging Coldhammer to push the travelers hard.

He went about his business as usual the rest of the day. He rode toward the north, away from the river, while still making his way westward. Here, too, he kept his eyes peeled for Indians. This was a land ranged by Cheyennes and Arapahos, Crows, Sioux, Shoshonis, even wandering bands of Blackfeet.

By the time evening was spreading over the land, Calhoun was tired and worn. It had been a long, hard two days, and he was glad to have found a good campsite for the wagons.

Since leaving Fort Laramie, the travelers had passed several more wagon trains. With each one they overtook, their choice of campsites became a little better. The ones Calhoun found for them often were unused, or at most lightly used. This one looked hardly touched.

CHAPTER

* 16 *

Calhoun wearily unsaddled the horse and began currying the animal. Despite his tiredness, he was relieved. He had been keenly alert for Indians throughout the long day. His relief came from not having seen any sign of hostiles in the area.

Not that he would get too lackadaisical, but he felt he could relax his ever-constant vigil a little.

He finished tending the horse, spending more time at it than usual. The horse had proved itself a worthy animal over the past two days, and deserved more care than normal.

Calhoun began gathering firewood. He was a little annoyed at himself for having fallen into doing this so regularly. Then he shrugged. The travelers had enough work to do each night in making camp, especially with the long hours Calhoun usually forced them to keep on the trail. He figured this little bit was the least he could do for them. Not that he would ever admit it.

He had a dozen small fires going, and wood piled next to each, when the first wagon rumbled into sight.

The travelers were not really all that surprised to

see Calhoun, considering that they had found his markers and the notes on the trail all day. Their only real surprise came from the fact that he had not met them the evening before.

Most of them were too tired, sore, and trail weary to care one way or the other, anyway. They were roused slightly, however, by seeing the fires blazing brightly in the dimming afternoon.

Camp was not long in being made, though the work never did cease. There was simply too much to do.

All the stock had to be watered and then brought out to where there was graze, if any. The harder-working animals had to be checked frequently to make sure yokes or harness were not chaffing, to make sure their shoes were still fitting properly and not worn too much. Cooking utensils had to be brought out and food prepared. Water barrels had to be filled. Wagons had to be checked and possibly repaired.

It was a never-ending litany of work and duties. It all too often left the people irritable and cross.

Calhoun sat off to the side a little, leaning back against his saddle. He watched with bored, dull eyes as the work progressed with as much smoothness as possible.

It never ceased to amaze him that out of such chaos could come a relatively peaceful camp in such a reasonably short time. That it happened usually was attributable to the quality of the wagon master. Calhoun had to admit a silent, grudging admiration for Barrett Coldhammer.

When the camp was finally made, Calhoun rose and strode to Coldhammer's fire. He squatted there, not evidencing the short spark of pain in his calf when the muscles stretched. He nodded in appreciation when Polly handed him a mug of hot, black coffee.

He sipped the thick, bitter liquid, watching Polly surreptitiously over the rim of the cup. She seemed to be giving him something of a cold shoulder, but he could not be sure.

Not that it mattered much. She had been a pleasant diversion. If that was to end, he figured, so be it. There was always Erline Rae, though he was not sure how she felt about him these days either. Granted, she had come to him that last night he was in camp, but after he had beaten her father, he was no longer sure about her.

If neither woman wanted anything to do with him any longer, he would survive. It was not as if he was in love with either. Still, such diversions always made the traveling easier.

Martha Coldhammer handed him a tin plate brimming with buffalo and potato stew. Two biscuits sat atop the stew. To Calhoun, who had not had a real meal since yesterday morning, the food's aroma was more than enticing. He dug in heartily.

To his right, a quarter of the way around the fire, Coldhammer did the same. Neither man had said anything. The two women soon served the rest of their family, then themselves. They sat back a little, away from the heat of the fire.

Calhoun and Coldhammer finished at about the

same time. They set their plates down. Calhoun reached into his shirt pocket for his cigarette fixings, but Coldhammer pulled out two cigars from his pocket and held one out toward Calhoun.

The guide took it and nodded. He bit off the end before shoving the cigar in his mouth. He grabbed a burning twig from the fire, held it out so Coldhammer could light his cigar, and then fired up his own.

"So, what happened?" Coldhammer finally asked. "You never did say in your notes."

Calhoun was not a man of many words. Quickly and without flourish, he explained the rudiments of his encounter with the Arapahos.

"How many of them was there?" Coldhammer asked. A pang of worry clutched at his insides.

"Five." Calhoun paused a heartbeat. "To start."

Coldhammer looked at him with an eyebrow raised in question.

"There was only three when they left off the attack," Calhoun said flatly.

Coldhammer nodded. Relief crept in to calm the worry. "They still lurkin' about?"

"Ain't seen hide nor hair of any 'Rapahos since. I ranged out a good spell and found no sign."

Coldhammer nodded again. He was completely relieved. He had encountered more than enough hostile Indians for one wagon trip already, as far as he was concerned.

The wagon master puffed on his cigar a little, stalling. Finally he said, "You know, Mister Calhoun, that some of the folks are talking poorly of you."

"How so?"

"Well," Coldhammer started, feeling the hesitancy rise again, "there's some said you didn't come back last night 'cause you was afraid." He held his breath, waiting for the expected explosion.

It did not come.

"Afraid of what?" Calhoun asked calmly.

Coldhammer gulped. This was getting harder, not easier. "Of Sherm North and his friends."

Calhoun nodded.

Coldhammer could not believe Calhoun was taking this all so calmly. From what the wagon master had seen in the month and a half or so Calhoun had been his guide, Calhoun had not shown a calm temper. Especially when it came to personal insults.

"That don't bother you?" Coldhammer asked softly. He had to ask, even at the risk of setting off the blast he still expected.

"Not when it comes from damn fools like Pepperdine or any of the others of that bunch."

"How'd you know it was them sayin' it?"

Calhoun shrugged. "Who else would it be?" Calhoun poured himself a little more coffee. "Cowards're usually the first to say that of others. I don't expect most folks'll listen to 'em."

If others did, he would deal with it when the time was right. However, he decided that he would have a chat with North, Pepperdine, and the others very soon.

Coldhammer sat quietly. He thought maybe he should say something about the other talk. He decided, however, that there was no point.

Sure, some of the people were making noise about the "trouble" Calhoun seemed to attract—or start—so easily. They were in the minority, though. Most of them were too-pious folk who were deeply offended not by Calhoun's violence but by his flouting of convention. His alleged cavorting with Erline Rae disturbed them.

Coldhammer had had plenty of reservations early on about having hired Calhoun. Those doubts had pretty well fled. The wagon master was glad most of the time that he had brought Calhoun along. Without the guide, the situation with Pepperdine's crew might have gotten well out of hand.

He watched as Calhoun finished his cigar and coffee.

Calhoun threw the butt into the fire and emptied his cup on the ground. He stood, stretching. Nodding good night, he headed toward his own little campsite. He was unconscious of the slight limp he used in favoring the wounded leg.

Coldhammer noticed it, though, and was surprised. He also thought the back of one of Calhoun's pants legs over the calf looked cut and soiled with dried blood.

Calhoun laid out his bedroll, wondering if he would be spending the night alone. Polly had offered no encouragement at supper, and he still did not know what Erline Rae was feeling about him after the other morning. Finally he shrugged and turned in, unconcerned.

He was only a little surprised when Polly slipped

into his bedroll well after the others had gone to sleep.

The fair young woman said nothing until afterward, when their breathing had come back to normal. Then she asked bluntly, "What do you see in that fallen woman, anyway?"

She had wondered that ever since she had found out, but she was too timid to ask. Finally she realized she had to know.

"That's none of your concern, ma'am," Calhoun answered evenly. He was not angry at the question, but he didn't think it deserved an answer.

"But . . .?"

"Hush," Calhoun said, placing a hard forefinger against Polly's soft lips. He sighed. Maybe some kind of answer would be appropriate. "You're different kinds of women," he offered.

"That's not hard to see," Polly said indignantly.

Calhoun smiled harshly into the darkness. So much for him trying to explain. "Just hush now," he added.

Polly grumbled a little, but then she snuggled closer to him, almost happy. Later they turned toward each other again.

At some point during the night, Calhoun ended up setting his wounded calf down on a small, sharp rock. He winced ever so briefly.

Polly looked at him in surprise. "Something wrong?" she asked, a little worried.

"No." He pulled her close again.

Polly would have none of it, though. She pulled back a little. "What's wrong?" she asked quietly but with determination.

Calhoun shrugged. "Took an arrow in the leg yesterday."

"Bad?" she asked.

"Nope."

She wasn't sure she believed him, but she had more urgent matters to attend to, and she gave in to her feelings.

Polly left well before dawn, hurrying quietly through the night toward her father's wagon.

Life returned to something resembling normalcy. For the next several days, Calhoun rode out and tended to his business like usual. He spent much of his time out there thinking, though.

It was clear that Polly had forgiven him. But he had hardly so much as caught a glance of Erline Rae. He did not think Erline Rae the kind of woman to hold what he had done to her father against him, and so he worried about her.

He had no chance to talk with her, though, even when he was in camp. After three days, he was considering just entering North's wagon and demanding to see her. That would cause a host of problems, he figured, but he didn't much care.

He helped Coldhammer and two other men repair a wagon. By the time that was finished, he was exhausted. He cleaned up a little and then turned in.

As Calhoun sat to breakfast the next morning, Coldhammer asked, "You think we could make it a short day today, Mister Calhoun?"

"Slackin' off, Mister Coldhammer?" Calhoun asked.

It had been said evenly, but Coldhammer thought he detected a note of warning in the words.

The wagon master grimaced. "Not to say slackin' off . . ." He paused. "The folks've been pushed hard from the start. It's beginnin' to tell on them."

"So?"

Coldhammer grew angry. He was not a coward, not by any means. He could not understand why he was so intimidated by Wade Calhoun, and that bothered him. Sure, Calhoun was an extraordinary gunman, and a man for whom spilling blood was a normal occurrence.

Still, Coldhammer had learned in the time Calhoun had been with him that Calhoun's violence was not random. It was well-directed, and always had a point. Coldhammer knew he had no reason to really fear Calhoun coming against him. Still, that knowledge was hard to translate into action.

Coldhammer fought back his anger. It would get him nowhere. Instead he said calmly, "Accordin' to my calculations, it's Independence Day, Mister Calhoun."

Calhoun was shocked by that information, and he wasn't sure why. Perhaps it was because he and Lizbeth . . .

He pushed that thought away right off. He nodded. "I suppose you were thinkin' of another fandango?" he asked. He was not all that displeased with the idea. Not that he wanted to take part, but he figured everyone, including himself, could use a small break.

"Well, I think the folks'd be happy to kick up their heels some."

Calhoun nodded. "I expect it won't set us back much," he allowed. He dumped out the dregs of his coffee. "But I'd best get movin'."

CHAPTER
* 17 *

There was a fine edge of excitement that afternoon when the wagons began pulling into the campsite Calhoun had selected. It was the earliest they had called it a day since they had left St. Joseph.

Even the labor of setting up camp seemed to go more quickly and smoothly. People worked with an almost joyous fervor.

The men tended the animals and saw to the wagons and heavy work.

The women, instead of just cooking supper for their families, got together in little groups to prepare food for a real feast for all. Before long, a variety of delicious aromas wafted over the camp, enticing even Calhoun.

While dark was still a couple of hours off, the food was laid out on long tables made of planks laid on barrels, chests, or other furniture.

Barrett Coldhammer rang a big iron triangle to get everyone's attention. He made a bland speech—one which Calhoun managed to avoid hearing by having urgent business behind some bushes.

Then Coldhammer offered up a short prayer of thanks for having been able to come so far with such little trouble, all things considered.

Finally, he grinned wide and shouted, "Food's on, folks."

There was a mad scramble for the food tables, with people jostling and shoving each other in friendly disputes.

Calhoun waited until the first wave was over before he moseyed to the makeshift tables. As he heaped a plate with foods—many carried from St. Joseph and saved for such an occasion—he noticed Rollie Pepperdine, Sherman North, Erline Rae, and the others standing by their wagons, waiting.

Calhoun was glad to at least see Erline Rae, and he decided that he would make an effort to talk with her sometime during the evening. She looked to be all right, if somewhat worn.

North looked fairly good, too, though he still wore most of the signs of Calhoun's beating.

Calhoun grinned tightly at the motley little group and finished filling his plate. He grabbed a mug of coffee and ambled toward a pile of rocks. He sat on one small boulder, set his plate and mug on another, and dug in.

As he ate, he watched the last stragglers, including Pepperdine's group, head for the waiting food. Calhoun half expected trouble to start, but no one did anything untoward.

Twenty minutes later, Calhoun was back at the tables, loading his plate again. He hadn't had a meal this good since he had been in St. Louis a few years ago, he thought.

As people began winding down their feasting, the

musicians began limbering up. Within minutes, the music was pouring forth into the new night. People began forming up and dancing.

Calhoun sat on his rock, watching the activity. He smoked, sipped coffee for a while, and tried to keep his mind off painful thoughts of the past.

Soon after, Coldhammer wandered up and sat on another rock next to Calhoun. He looked around, as if making sure no one was looking. He pulled a small bottle of whiskey from inside his shirt and held it toward Calhoun.

"I don't usually approve of such things at a fandango like this," Coldhammer said calmly. "Too often leads to troubles."

He paused as Calhoun took the bottle.

"But I expect you're a man who can hold himself in check," Coldhammer said. He stood. "Well, enjoy the evening, Mister Calhoun." He walked off.

Calhoun watched the wagon master's back dwindle for a moment. Then he eased the cork out of the bottle. He held the bottle up and took a long swallow.

The whiskey was cheap and harsh, biting its way down his throat. Calhoun thought it tasted just fine.

Calhoun relaxed, pulling from the bottle and puffing on hand-rolled cigarettes. He almost began to enjoy himself as he watched the people whirling and stomping around the clearing that served as a dance floor.

The bottle didn't last long. He tossed it aside, regretting a little that it was gone, but then he shrugged. Better not to have too much. He did not need to be three sheets to the wind when he went to talk with Erline Rae.

He decided he ought to do it soon, since dark had fallen, but it could wait a little while yet. Especially since Erline Rae was being hauled around the dance area almost constantly by one or the other of Pepperdine's crew.

Calhoun watched Polly for a while. She, too, had no chance to sit down, as she was in constant demand by nearly every man on the wagon train. Watching her, Calhoun felt the pangs of a life lost.

He shook off the spreading gloom of his thoughts. Crushing out another cigarette, he stood up. It was about time, he decided, to pay a visit to Erline Rae. Especially seeing as how Pepperdine and his companions had gotten a goodly supply of whiskey and were not being shy in making it dwindle.

A song ended. As the musicians took a short break to grab a swallow of whiskey or water and decide on the next tune, Calhoun walked slowly toward North's wagon.

None of the six men, nor Erline Rae, spotted Calhoun until he was there. By then, the music had begun again. Bass Cutler grabbed Erline Rae's arm and started pulling her toward the dance area.

He stopped when he almost ran into Calhoun, who had planted himself in front of the fat man.

"My turn with Miss Erline," Calhoun said quietly.

"Get the hell out of my way," Cutler snapped, glowering. He put a flabby hand on Calhoun's chest and shoved. Calhoun did not move.

Cutler shoved again with no more results than before. "Move, damnit," he growled, trying to do verbally what he could not do physically.

"I reckon not," Calhoun said quietly.

Cutler's eyes grew large, and he looked down. Unbeknownst to him, Calhoun had drawn his big Bowie knife. The tip of the sharp blade rested on Cutler's trousers, a hand's breadth below the belt buckle.

Cutler gulped.

"Miss Erline," Calhoun said, "I'd be obliged for your company a spell."

She said nothing. She just smiled in relief and jerked her wrist from Cutler's fat, sweaty grip. Erline Rae moved to Calhoun's side.

"I don't expect you boys to trouble us," Calhoun warned.

He slid the knife away, took Erline Rae's damp palm in his hand, and strolled away, seemingly unconcerned. His other hand did hover near the butt of one of his Colt Dragoons, though.

They reached Calhoun's bedroll, which he had nestled in among some brush. It was hidden from the revelry by the brush and the night.

Erline Rae laughed softly, in relief. She turned to face Calhoun. "Lord, am I glad you come to fetch me," she said fervently.

Calhoun nodded and almost smiled. "How come you never come to visit?" he asked quietly.

Erline Rae licked her lips nervously. Her eyes flickered in the darkness, looking back toward her wagon. Calhoun didn't see it, but he did notice her quickened breath.

"Pa and the others wouldn't let me," she said. The fright and resignation in her voice were unmistakable.

"There was always at least one of them with me." Her voice caught. "He even tied me to him nights."

"You ain't mad at me for whuppin' your old man a few days ago?"

"Lord no. I . . ." She wanted to tell him that she wished he had killed her father, but she could not bring herself to verbalize it.

Calhoun nodded. He understood, but he could not see any reason to say anything.

"I'd like to go back," Erline Rae said quietly.

"To your wagon?" Calhoun asked. He was surprised.

"No," Erline Rae said with a sigh of contentment. "Back to the dance."

Calhoun nodded. He had no desire to get up out of the comfortable bedroll and don his clothes again. But if Erline Rae wanted it, he would agree.

They rose and dressed without hurry. Then they strolled back toward where the dancing was still in full progress. They stood to the side watching a little.

Something bothered Calhoun, but he wasn't sure what it was.

One of Lije Wilkins's sons moseyed up. Stammering, he shyly asked Erline Rae to dance.

Erline Rae looked at Calhoun, who nodded. He did not dance, and he wanted some peace to try to figure out what was nudging his unconscious.

Erline Rae and the suddenly proud Lee Wilkins headed away.

Calhoun stood, eyes scanning the people, the wagons, the brush as far as he could see in the light of the many fires. Something was not right; he just knew it.

Then it dawned on him. He did not see North, Tiny Bates, and Bass Cutler. Pepperdine and the other two of his ilk were sitting on barrels near Pepperdine's wagon, but the others were not in sight.

Calhoun faded into the darkness behind him. Then he skirted the camp, until he came up on North's and Pepperdine's wagons. The music was still playing, and the three men were still sitting there watching it.

Silently, Calhoun climbed up into Pepperdine's wagon, through the front. He made a quick look around. North and the other two were not there. He slipped out and made his way to North's wagon, which was just ahead of Pepperdine's.

He also climbed into that one and searched it quickly. There was no one inside.

Outside, he stood in the shadows, once more scanning the camp. He was bothered more than ever at not having found the three men. He was certain they were up to some mischief.

Making it worse was the fact that he sensed something else was not right. As he watched the dancing, he had the germ of an idea. He didn't like it the least little bit, either.

He moved back and started moving soundlessly around the perimeter of the camp again, aiming to complete the circle he had started.

He hadn't gone far when he heard Bates's high-pitched, wild giggle, quickly stifled. He thought he also heard a whimper of fear.

Anger seared across Calhoun's eyes. Moving cautiously through the darkness, he pulled a Dragoon. The sounds grew more regular and more evident. He nodded.

Pale moonlight filtered down, illuminating a small break in the brush. Hardly breathing, Calhoun stopped and surveyed the scene for a moment.

He stepped out of the brush. In less than two strides, he was behind Cutler. His left hand snaked out and grabbed Cutler's pistol. Before the fat man could react, Calhoun had slapped the barrel of Cutler's revolver against his head.

Cutler collapsed.

North was occupied with trying to strip a struggling young woman. Bates was busy watching and giggling maniacally. Neither even knew Calhoun was there.

Until Calhoun knelt alongside the woman and stuck the muzzle of his pistol in North's ear.

"I expect it'll upset Miz Wright here somethin' awful was I to splatter your brains all over her," Calhoun said quietly.

The words sent a chill up North's spine.

"That is," Calhoun added, "if you got any."

Calhoun was aware of Bates behind him. "I'd think mighty poorly of Mister Bates bein' the cause of my demise, was I you," Calhoun offered.

Bates stopped moving.

"Now, suppose you stand up, nice and slow."

North did as he was told, Calhoun moving with him.

Without having North laying atop her, Clair

Wright scrambled up and ran, screaming, toward the dance.

"Both of you grab your lard-ass partner there."

North and Bates helped haul a moaning Cutler to his feet.

"March." Calhoun wiggled the pistol toward the main part of camp.

"You're makin' a mistake, Calhoun," North growled. "A big mistake."

"Shut your yap and move. Unless you'd like to make your peace right here and now."

The three shuffled off ahead of Calhoun, who walked slowly behind them, pistol at the ready.

The music had stopped by the time they entered the camp, and a group of men was heading toward them.

Clair was near Coldhammer's wagon, being comforted by a number of the women.

Erline Rae stood off to the side, looking ashamed, and very alone.

CHAPTER

* 18 *

The music had scraped to a halt, and quiet fell over the camp; a hush broken only by small, easy sounds. A babe cried for a moment before mother's milk calmed and silenced him. The fires crackled and snapped, sending up small bursts of sparks. Women's voices carried softly on the night air as they tried to soothe a sobbing Clair Wright.

The men slowed as they neared Calhoun and his three prisoners. All the male travelers were armed, as they had been since the beginning. Out here a dance was no excuse for leaving one's arms in the wagon.

Several of the men veered off and headed for Pepperdine's wagon. Without making a show of it, they brought weapons to bear on Pepperdine, Billy Quince, and Chuck Dillard.

Coldhammer stopped a few feet in front of Cutler, whose massive obesity was still being supported by North and Bates. The two men were struggling to keep their corpulent friend up.

Coldhammer looked to be holding himself on a tight rein. The men lumped behind him seemed little more friendly.

"Explain," Coldhammer snapped.

"I don't know what you mean, Cap'n," North said unctuously.

"Bates?"

"I don't know nuttin' neither," Bates said nasally.

Coldhammer looked at Calhoun. "Miz Wright's gibberin'. Ain't surprisin', I suppose. But it's mighty hard to make out what she's sayin'."

He paused to cut a wad of chew and stuff it in his cheek. "I did catch that it had somethin' to do with Mister North and his cronies here. You know anything about it, Mister Calhoun?"

"Not too much." He almost smiled when he saw North's tense back relax a little. "All I know is that I come upon Sherm here lyin' atop Miz Wright—who was strugglin' somethin' fierce. He was tryin' to tear her clothes off. The other two were eggin' him on."

Coldhammer's face was a study of rage.

"I wasn't doin' nothin' of the sort," North snapped, trying to raise some indignation. He licked his lips. He didn't often think before he acted, and it frequently got him into trouble. He was trying to think now, though, to come up with something that would rebuff the wall of hate that had grown in front of him.

"It was him," North suddenly blurted. He jerked a thumb over his shoulder at Calhoun. "Yeah, it was him."

He couldn't hold Cutler any longer. He looked at Bates and nodded. The two men slipped out from under Cutler's weight. Cutler hovered there a moment on his feet before falling. No one paid him any heed.

"It was him tryin' to defile that nice Miz Wright." North was sweating. He was not at all certain that anyone would believe him, especially if the woman had talked any. He felt he had to try, though.

"Me and Tiny and Bass there heard some noise out in the bushes. It sounded like . . . well . . ." He tried to chuckle in manly camaraderie. It came out sounding like a death rattle.

The pseudo-laughter ground down. North coughed in embarrassment. Then he went on, voice quavering. "Me, Tiny, and Bass went off to see what was goin' on. We found him"—again the thumb over the shoulder—"tryin' to molest that poor young—"

"Stop!"

Everyone turned his head to look at Erline Rae. She stood there, defiance covering her darkly beautiful face.

"You just stop your lyin'," she said sharply, edging up a little. She had never even thought of doing something like this before, and she was scared.

"Shut your mouth, daughter," North snarled. His demeanor has lost all semblance of friendliness.

"Or what?" she demanded. She moved a little closer, gaining strength. "There ain't nothin' you can do to me now that you ain't put me through ten times worse already."

She paused, worried that she might have said too much. She knew tongues had been wagging about her since they left Missouri. This was the first time those rumors had been given any credence, though. She hoped not too much credence.

North's lips flapped, but no sounds emerged.

"Mister North?" Coldhammer said icily. He had had about his fill of Sherman North and the others.

"Who're you gonna believe, damnit?" North demanded, growing angry. "Me or that worthless trollop?"

Calhoun, who had long ago put his Colt Dragoon back in his holster, slammed North in the back of the head with a forearm. North fell forward onto his knees.

Calhoun reached down, grabbed North by the back of the shirt, and hauled him to his feet again. "Watch your mouth," he warned tightly.

"Get your goddamn hands away from me," North snarled, slapping at Calhoun and trying to jerk free.

Calhoun finally let him go.

"Is there any truth in what Mister North said, Mister Calhoun?" Coldhammer asked. He was certain he knew the answer, especially after the little bit of information he had gleaned from among Clair's babble. Still, he wanted to be as fair as possible.

"What do you think?" Calhoun said nonchalantly.

Coldhammer nodded. "I told you more than once, Mister North, that your shenanigans would bring you no end of grief if they were to continue. After this, I'm afraid I'm going to have to put you and your two friends in irons for the rest of the journey."

"Like hell you will," North snarled. His anger was beginning to overwhelm him.

"Such talk'll only make things worse."

North sputtered a few times before he could form words. "You can't do this, Cap'n. Not on his word."

He pointed a withering finger at Calhoun. He was beside himself with anger, and knew he had nothing more to lose.

Sherman North had developed a deep-seated hatred for Calhoun since the beginning. Calhoun's having beaten Rollie Pepperdine to a pulp a couple of times served to solidify his hate.

But what had really pushed him over the edge was Calhoun's affair with Erline Rae. North had suspected it for a while, but was not sure until just recently. Since then, he wanted to get Calhoun. When Calhoun had taken Erline Rae away from him, he had snapped.

Then he had spotted Clair. It did not take long to convince Bates and Cutler to join him in grabbing the widow and dragging her into the bushes.

Calhoun had even ruined that for him. Now North was in a rage.

"Hell, he's even got my daughter lyin' against me to save his hide," North ranted.

"And just how would he do that, Mister North?" Coldhammer asked. His attitude had not softened any.

"You know," North said, his words weasely sounding.

"No, I don't." Coldhammer moved toward North. "Now, I told you that if you was to cause trouble again, I'd put an end to it."

"Damnit, I've told you I ain't done nothin' wrong. It was him. Calhoun." He was shouting and raving, not making much sense. "He ruint my baby girl."

"Stop your babblin'," Coldhammer said harshly.

He stopped directly in front of North. "You're makin' a spectacle of yourself, and not makin' sense."

"If you won't do nothin' about him after he ruint my daughter, then, damnit, I will." He shoved Coldhammer, trying to knock him out of the way.

The wagon master was not so easily moved. "I don't cotton to bein' taken lightly, North," he said sharply, knocking the arm down and away.

"Goddamnit, Coldhammer, either you finish it, or let me do it."

Coldhammer stood silently, thinking. He had enough sense—even if North didn't—to know North had no chance in a gunfight against a man like Calhoun. Besides, Coldhammer didn't really want any killing here.

On the other hand, North and his pals had caused more than a little trouble, and there was no end to it in sight. If Coldhammer put North in irons, someone would have to watch him, as well as the others in his group.

If he let North challenge Calhoun, at least here and now it would be out in the open. If he didn't let this proceed, it most likely would end up with a bushwhacking. Innocent people could be hurt—possibly killed—that way. He picked what he figured was the lesser of the two evils.

"You got any objections, Mister Calhoun?" Coldhammer asked over North's shoulder. He never took his eyes from North.

"Nope."

"It ought to be a fair fight, North," Coldhammer suggested. He had little hope that it would be followed, since Calhoun had already whaled the tar out of North. He had to try, though. "I'd as soon like to see that no guns or knives were involved."

"Just get yourself out of the way, Coldhammer," North snapped. He, too, remembered the beating. He hitched up his gun belt, which had sagged considerably, and walked past Coldhammer, wanting a little distance between himself and Calhoun behind him.

Coldhammer felt he had to give it one more try. "You're gonna get yourself killed, North," he commented. He realized he was almost looking forward to it, if only as a way to stop all the trouble.

"That's none of your concern," North said. He licked his lips. Some of the reality of this situation was beginning to dawn on him, and he started to worry. Talking big was easy. But going against a man like Calhoun was another story altogether.

He knew, though, that he had gone too far to back down. If he did that now, he would look like a fool. He was sure he could not live with the scorn.

Coldhammer stared at North a moment, knowing he was looking at a dead man. He shrugged. It was out of his hands. He stepped aside silently.

The other men began backing away, moving toward the wagons on the side of what had so recently been a dance floor.

Calhoun stood loosely, unworried. His thumbs were hooked lightly in the front of his gun belt, his right hand within inches of the Dragoons.

North was tense, his posture rigid. He licked his lips and looked around at the people. He found little sympathy.

"Your call, North," Calhoun said quietly.

"Son of a bitch," North screamed. His hand flew to the butt of his pistol and he yanked. The revolver caught on the cracked leather holster and North panicked. He glanced down, still jerking at his worn five-shot Colt Paterson.

Calhoun watched, feeling neither sympathy nor disgust. He could have easily whipped out one of his Dragoons and drilled North while the man struggled to free his pistol. But Calhoun's streak of perversity reared up again, and so he waited.

"Take your time," he called. A sardonic grin curled the corners of his thin lips. It was lost in the darkness.

That only angered North all the more. In his rage, he encountered more difficulty drawing his weapon. But finally the old Colt was in his hand. He snapped back the hammer and let a shot fly. The ball kicked up dirt halfway between him and Calhoun.

A few uneasy chuckles surfaced from the people watching from behind or inside wagons.

Infuriated, North jerked the weapon higher in his shaky hand and fired again. Once more the bullet fell far short.

He fired again twice more. One bullet hit a tree a dozen yards to Calhoun's left; the other whined off a rock. North began to sweat. He had only one more shot left, since he usually carried all five chambers loaded.

Calhoun calmly drew a Dragoon. "You had your chance," he said quietly as the hammer clicked back to full cock.

He fired once.

A woman screamed as a hole suddenly appeared in North's forehead and the back of the man's head exploded. North's body stood, weaving. He was dead, but the information had not registered on his burst brain yet.

Then North crumpled without a sound. He lay in a heap. People began edging out of their havens and stared at him silently.

Calhoun holstered his pistol, turned a little, and glared at Bates and Cutler. The fat man had managed to get to his feet. He and his diminutive friend had scrambled out of the way.

"Either of you boys like a dose?" Calhoun asked calmly.

The two men were chalky, except where the fires reddened their faces. Both shook their heads vigorously.

"I'd be obliged was we to have no more trouble out of you two—and those varmints over there." He pointed toward Pepperdine, Dillard, and Quince.

CHAPTER

∗ 19 ∗

W hile some men carted North's body off, Calhoun went to Erline Rae.

"You all right?" he asked.

She nodded. She did not look upset; only a little shocked. That mainly was from the realization that she was free for the first time in her life.

"Let's go."

"Where?" Erline Rae asked, surprised.

"You'll see." Calhoun took Erline Rae's arm and walked with head held high across the camp toward North's wagon.

Polly saw it, and her heart sank. Many of the others watched, too, with varying degrees of disgust. Most of the women did not understand how Calhoun and Erline Rae could flaunt their lack of convention. They clicked their tongues and murmured.

Polly would have none of it. Whatever she might think of Erline Rae, it was apparent to her that Calhoun cared at least somewhat for the dark-haired beauty. That might make her jealous, but it didn't make her hate Calhoun, or Erline Rae, either. She softly scolded the muttering women, showing her displeasure. She might have a made a few enemies with it, but she felt better for having done it.

Calhoun climbed into North's wagon and set match to the lantern. Then he held out his hand for Erline Rae. She followed him up.

"What's yours in here?" Calhoun asked.

"Not much," Erline Rae admitted. She suddenly felt ashamed.

"Anything that ain't yours or your old man's, pitch outside." He paused. "Anything of your pa's, too, if you got no use for it."

Erline Rae looked at him, still a little dazed at all that had happened in just the past few minutes.

"This is your wagon now, Erline," Calhoun said quietly. "You don't have to have nothin' in it you don't want."

"But, what about Tiny and Bass?" Erline Rae shuddered at the thought of the fat slob and the maniacal little man.

"They won't be travelin' with you no more," Calhoun said flatly. He paused. "'Less'n you want 'em to."

"Good Lord, no!" Erline Rae breathed, suppressing another shudder.

"Then pitch their stuff. They want it, they'll round it up. They don't, it'll stay there."

"How'll they travel?" Erline Rae still couldn't believe she was unfettered.

Calhoun shrugged. "Ain't my concern. Or yours."

Erline Rae giggled. Relief didn't wash over her suddenly. It was more like a long, slow buildup that inched through her veins. She was beginning to see some of the possibilities. Some of the problems, too, but those she would deal with later.

Calhoun half smiled. "You point and I'll pitch."

Erline Rae giggled again and pointed to a trunk. "Tiny's," she said. She did not shudder this time simply at mentioning the name.

Calhoun nodded. He heaved the trunk out the back of the wagon. It landed with a crash, almost on Bates, who was peering into the back of the wagon.

"Hey, goddamnit," Bates shouted. "That's my things."

"I know," Calhoun allowed.

"But . . ." He paused, trying to collect his few wits. "Sherm said anything was to happen to him, the wagon was mine." He leered. "And I was to be Erline's guardian."

"Buffalo shit." He grabbed another trunk Erline Rae had pointed to and threw that. He made an effort to hit Bates.

The little man barely skipped out of the way. "Hey, you can't do that."

Calhoun heaved an old saddle.

"Damnit, I'll . . ."

Calhoun stood, not even breathing hard despite the exertion. His thumbs were hooked loosely on his gun belt. "You'll what?" he asked calmly.

Bates might be half crazy, but he could see his own death in Calhoun's dark eyes. "Nuttin'," he mumbled.

"Didn't think so." Calhoun grabbed a burlap sack of clothes and threw it out. "I reckon you and lard belly out there ought to go kiss Pepperdine's ass and see if he'll take you on in his wagon."

Bates said nothing, but his eyes screamed out his

desire to kill Calhoun. He turned after a moment and began gathering up his belongings.

"Come on, damnit, Bass, get your fat ass over here and get your stuff. I ain't gonna take it over to Rollie's for you."

Calhoun almost hit Coldhammer with his next toss. He shrugged by way of apology.

Coldhammer nodded. "You two comin' to the buryin'?" he asked.

"Not me," Calhoun said. He had no reason to. Sherman North had been nothing to him, and he could not see standing around trying to look remorseful for having just killed a man he barely knew and cared about even less.

"Miss Erline?" Calhoun asked, turning to look at her.

She shook her head, some of her old fears returning.

"I understand, ma'am," Coldhammer said. He wasn't sure he really did understand, but he could sympathize. Rumors had been rampant since Missouri about what went on in the North wagon.

"I wasn't the wagon master, I wouldn't be goin' either," he added. He touched the brim of his hat in saying goodbye to Erline Rae. Then he turned and walked away.

Erline Rae felt relief again. With renewed spirits, she went back to directing Calhoun in ridding the wagon of unwanted goods and supplies.

Finally they were done. By then the camp was quiet for the most part. The dance had ended with the trouble, and now that the burying was over, most of the people had turned in.

Erline Rae and Calhoun looked around the wagon. It was nearly empty, considering the jumble of things that had been there to start with. Erline Rae was pleased with the neatness.

"Well, ma'am, I'd best get some shut-eye," Calhoun said politely.

"Don't go."

He had been almost certain that she would invite him to stay. However, he had wanted to give her the chance of getting out of it gracefully, should she desire to.

"You sure?" he asked.

"Yes." She came up to him and wrapped her arms around his waist. His pistols dug into her midsection, but she did not care. She hugged him hard. Calhoun held her. He knew she needed him, not only as a man, but for the protection he offered. Pepperdine and the others would not do anything to her while he was around.

In the morning, he ate his breakfast at Erline Rae's fire. He paid no more attention to the disapproving glances he received from the women than he did to the hate-filled stares Pepperdine's crew gave him.

Coldhammer strolled up just after Calhoun had finished eating. He squatted by the fire and poured coffee for himself. Calhoun nodded hello.

"You going to be on the job today?" Coldhammer asked.

"No reason not to."

Coldhammer nodded. "Thought you might think of one." He glanced over the coffee cup at Erline Rae.

"That is a concern," Calhoun allowed. "I'd be obliged if you was to have somebody drive the wagon for her; maybe watch over her while I'm out."

He hated to ask a favor of anyone. He assuaged his conscience by telling himself silently that this was asked not for him, but for Erline Rae.

"I expect Lije's oldest boy—Lee—will be more than happy to oblige." He grinned.

Calhoun smiled as much as he ever did. He knew that Lee Wilkins was sweet on Erline Rae. He also knew he had no competition from the boy.

"You'll be pushin' on soon, Mister Calhoun?" Coldhammer asked. He stood and dumped the bitter dregs of his coffee out.

"Yep."

"I'll send Lee over directly." Coldhammer left.

By the time Calhoun had finished his second leisurely cup of coffee, Wilkins arrived.

The young man had scrubbed his face and slicked down his hair. His clothing was worn but as clean and neat as he could make them. "I'm obliged you sought my services, ma'am," he said, voicing cracking with embarrassment.

"My pleasure to have you here, Mister Wilkins," Erline Rae said. She felt funny. Not many men had shown her much respect in life. Calhoun had been one, but it was a rough-hewn respect, not this schoolboy respect mixed with a good dose of discomfit. Making it all the more strange, was that Wilkins was so sincere about it.

Wilkins wandered off and began preparing the harness.

Calhoun stood. With a half-smile, he said to Erline Rae, "Best watch out for that boy, or you'll be headin' to a preacher before you know it."

Erline Rae laughed with a newfound shyness. The very thought was ridiculous.

Minutes later, he had saddled his horse and rode out, towing a mule behind him.

He followed the well-worn trail along the Sweetwater River that skirted the Antelope Hills. Though it was imperceptible, Calhoun knew that the trail was heading ever upward, toward the long, gentle slope of South Pass.

He had hoped to be at or through South Pass by now, but with two days spent at Fort Laramie and then the celebration last night, they had not made it. He thought that with a real long day and no trouble, they might make the forty miles or so to the pass. He didn't think it very likely, really, but it didn't hurt anyone to hope for it.

He was constantly on the alert for Indians, considering his brush with the Arapahos not so long ago. He saw no one, though, either red or white.

He did, however, find a small herd of buffalo grazing on the rough grass later in the afternoon. He took one and butchered out the hump meat and ribs and some of the other meat. Wrapping the bloody flesh in pieces of hide, he loaded it on the mule.

As he worked, Calhoun kept a practiced eye turned on the bunched clouds gathering to the northwest and blowing toward them. As he finished packing the meat, he judged the rain would start in about three hours—just after dark.

Calhoun moved on, looking for a decent campsite for the night. He knew now that the pass was beyond reach for this night. They would have to stop before nightfall unless they wanted to make camp in the dark and rain.

There was little in the way of cover out on the rugged high country. He finally settled for a spot on a long, flat-topped ridge. It was close enough to the river to have water available, but not so close to be a danger. If the rains that were coming turned out to be heavy, the travelers would not want to be caught too close to the river, which might flood.

Nor would they want to camp in a low spot. Such a place could turn into a raging, churning torrent full of debris within minutes.

The rain was coming down steadily as the first wagons pulled to a stop at the site. None of the emigrants was happy with Calhoun's choice of campsites, but Calhoun just shrugged. He figured they could always go look for another spot should they be real unhappy with it.

There was no wood for the cookfires, but there were buffalo chips in abundance. The flat slabs of old, dried buffalo dung burned quickly, but they burned hot. And they added a certain tanginess to the food cooked over them.

Calhoun tried to ignore the chilling rain that soaked through his threadbare hat, coat, and shirt. He usually took rain as he took everything else—

with a fatalistic acceptance. For some reason, though, this rain irritated him.

He spit his annoyance into a puddle as he unsaddled his horse and rubbed the animal down. Then he headed off to talk with Coldhammer. He wanted to see how the day had gone for the travelers.

The Coldhammer family had a fire going off the side of the wagon. It was protected by an old tarp. The canvas top of the wagon was rolled up on that side so that food could be passed up to the people inside without anyone having to get wet.

Coldhammer looked harried, so Calhoun opted not to bother the man. He headed to supper with Erline Rae.

CHAPTER

✳ 20 ✳

Lee Wilkins was none too pleased when Calhoun returned. The young man had rigged a tarp on Erline Rae's wagon, like the one on Coldhammer's. He had thought perhaps he would have a little more time with Erline Rae.

Wilkins shuffled off unhappily, his hurt feelings salvaged only by the warm smile of thanks Erline Rae gave him.

Calhoun took his plate of fresh buffalo meat mixed with beans, and his cup of coffee. He looked for a spot that might be relatively comfortable. He didn't see any.

Erline Rae insisted they sit up in the wagon. Without Bates's and Cutler's belongings, there was plenty of space. They would be dry, warm, and cozy.

While Erline Rae cleaned up after supper, Calhoun slogged through the mud to Coldhammer's wagon. He plopped down on an old trunk Coldhammer had set out near the fire, and he poured himself coffee.

Coldhammer climbed down out of the wagon and joined him. He handed Calhoun a cigar. In a moment, both men were puffing.

"Any troubles today?" Calhoun asked.

"None that I could see." He grimaced through the

cloud of cigar smoke. "Not even from Pepperdine and that bunch."

"They'll try somethin'. Sooner or later."

"I know." He paused. "I just wish I knew when."

Calhoun shrugged.

"You see anything out there?"

"Not a soul."

"Reckon that's good."

"I expect." Calhoun was especially glad he had seen no fresh sign of Indians. He had no real desire to see any more wagon trains, either, for that matter. People only brought trouble.

They sat silently, smoking, for a while. Finally Calhoun stood and walked off. There was nothing more to say, and so no reason to linger.

Erline Rae had a hard night. It seemed to Calhoun as if everything was finally catching up to her. The night before had been one filled with wonder at the thought of being free at last. The worries and doubts and fears had waited twenty-four hours before appearing.

She tossed and turned. Several times she moaned in her restless half sleep, seemingly unaware that she was doing so.

Calhoun did what little he could for her. He had never been comfortable in such situations, even with Lizbeth. He held Erline Rae as tight as he dared, half afraid he would break her, trying to prevent her thrashing around. After several hours, it seemed it helped, since she began to calm down.

Calhoun's night was no more comfortably spent than Erline Rae's, considering that she kept him awake through most of it. He only settled down when she did.

As usual, he was up before the others. He could not tell whether it was really still night, or whether the cloudiness and gloom would not let the beginning of dawn through.

By the time he had finished taking care of his personal business, Erline Rae was up and stoking up last night's fire. She smiled wanly as Calhoun came up and started helping her.

Before long they had finished their meal. Erline Rae felt a little better after having eaten. She grinned at Calhoun. "Gave you a hard time last night, didn't I?" she asked softly.

Calhoun shrugged. He had had worse ones.

"I can maybe make it up to you." Her eyes held his without shame. She smiled.

"Wouldn't hurt," he allowed.

They climbed into the wagon and lowered the canvas side again.

Just after they finished, they heard someone rattling harness chains. They arose, straightened themselves, and climbed down.

Lee Wilkins glowered at Calhoun for a moment before dropping his gaze, suddenly afraid at the threat in Calhoun's dark eyes.

Calhoun swaggered off toward his horse, carrying his saddle. The rain still fell in buckets, annoying him. He did not look forward to a long day on horseback in the downpour.

He thought he made it through South Pass about noon. It was hard to tell the pass under the best of circumstances, so gentle was it. Figuring out the time of day was tricky, too, considering the dingy grayness of the day.

Three miles northwest of the pass, taking the Sublette Cutoff, he came to Pacific Springs. He pulled up and looked around.

He saw no signs that the place had been used recently. He had wondered about that. Calhoun had been there several times in the past, and knew it was a favorite stopping place for wagon trains and Army columns.

The rain had eased but not stopped. It was going to be hellacious enough for the wagons to get even this far. So, even though it was still awhile before real darkness fell, he decided this was far enough for one day.

Pacific Springs was more than just a spring. Under normal circumstances, it was a marsh. Now, it was nearly a lake. A shallow lake, maybe, but a lake nonetheless.

He had seen horses and oxen bog down here before. It would be tricky getting the wagons across the area with all the rain they had had. It seemed to stretch on to forever from Calhoun's left to right. There was no apparent way to go around.

Calhoun thought of taking a short break to eat some buffalo jerky. He decided, though, that there would be no comfort in such a poor meal while sitting here in the open.

He spent some time, however, in looking the land over from his horse's back. He was trying to find the most likely spot to cross the quagmire.

He figured he would have to guess ultimately, since he could not see the treacherous mud beneath the grass. The herbage seemed to be almost floating. The horses would have good eating.

He decided not to try to make it across now. Better they should camp here, on this side for the night. It might be taking a risk. If the rains kept up, the marsh might be almost impassable by morning. On the other hand, it would be easier tackling the difficult crossing in the morning when the animals were strong and fresh.

He dismounted and pulled off the saddle. He found some bushes and shoved the saddle into them as far as he could. He pulled a large, thin rubber sheet from a saddlebag. He pulled it over the bush and held the corners down with rocks.

Then he went searching for hunks of sage that might have stayed dry under bushes. He found some and kept carrying it back and stuffing it under the rubber sheet.

When he finished, figuring he had enough, he was soaked with sweat and rain. He sat, heedless of the rain. He fought off sleep.

Before he could become too bored, or too annoyed from sitting in the rain, the wagons appeared on the gray horizon. The rain had slackened off some more but still showed no signs of stopping.

As the wagon train neared, Calhoun moved out a ways. He wanted them to pull off and to the side long before they hit the bog. He could see Lije Wilkins turn in his seat on the lead wagon. Wilkins's voice came faintly to Calhoun, calling for Cold-hammer.

Coldhammer trotted up, and stopped. He looked where Wilkins was pointing toward Calhoun.

Coldhammer galloped forward and pulled up sharply in front of Calhoun.

As the wagon master slid off the horse, Calhoun knew right off there was trouble. He could see it in the wagon master's face.

"Tell it," he said, before Coldhammer had both feet on the ground.

"Pepperdine and his crew are gone," Coldhammer said flatly.

"So?" That could not be bothering Coldhammer.

"They took Clair Wright." He paused an instant, looking into Calhoun's deep eyes. "And Erline Rae."

Calhoun's eyes clouded over with rage. Everything that he was told him to saddle his horse and ride out after them. Only his common sense kept him from moving.

"When?" he asked tightly.

"Half-hour or so after you pulled out."

"Why didn't you send somebody out for me right after?" Calhoun was trying to keep his always volatile temper in check.

"Couldn't." Coldhammer spit. He was sick inside about it. There was nothing they could have done, and that made him squirm. Calhoun's look made him feel worse.

Calhoun figured Coldhammer must have a reason for it, and he knew he would learn it sooner or later. He noted that Wilkins's wagon was almost on them.

"Shit," he muttered. "I was plannin' to stay this side of the marsh tonight. But maybe we'd best get to the other side."

"Why?"

"I aim to get on their trail soon's I can. It'd be best was I to be here to help you across."

Coldhammer nodded. "Where?"

"Over there," Calhoun said, pointing. "I think." He hadn't tried it, not thinking it would be necessary to cross so soon. He headed for his saddle.

A few minutes later, he was edging the animal into the swirling water over a layer of treacherous muck. The water was cold, and clear, as far as he could tell.

Coldhammer sat on his own horse at the edge of the morass, watching alertly.

Calhoun made it across safely, though there were a few tense moments. He came back a little more quickly.

With Calhoun on one side of Wilkins's wagon and Coldhammer on the other, they guided the first wagon across.

It took more than four hours to get all the wagons and extra stock across the wide marsh. By then it was dark.

They had lost an ox and a horse in the doing. Both animals had wandered off the obscure trail, almost as if together. In moments they were mired in the mud. By the time the men could mount something of a rescue effort, both animals had sunk almost to their snouts. Calhoun shot both to end their torment.

The travelers were a dull and dismal group as they set up the camp. The people were soaked through and covered with mud. They were irritable, and tended to take it out on each other.

Most had had sense enough to collect buffalo chips when it had been convenient and store the fuel in boxes under the wagons. Plus there was the sage that Calhoun had gathered earlier. Fires were soon started and food set to cooking.

Calhoun ate at Coldhammer's fire, like in the old days. The family ate up inside the wagon. Calhoun was in no mood for company, so he just took his plate of boiled buffalo and potatoes and his cup of black coffee and scrunched under the wagon to eat.

The ground was no more dry under there than it was anywhere else. Calhoun didn't much care anyway; his pants were so wet already that he could have sat in a lake and been none the worse for it.

Polly came to sit with him for a while—until her father called her back to join the rest of the family.

Polly glanced around, making sure that no one was looking. Then she quickly, hungrily kissed Calhoun on the mouth. With a feeling of satisfaction, she climbed back up inside the wagon.

Calhoun moved out from under the prairie schooner, and sat back against one of the wheels, still under the tarp.

Coldhammer arrived just after, and squatted near him. He pulled a small bottle of whiskey from inside his shirt and held it out.

Moments later, several men—including Lije and Lee Wilkins—joined the two.

Calhoun took a long pull at the whiskey and handed it back to Coldhammer. "Tell it," he ordered.

CHAPTER

✳ 21 ✳

"**P**epperdine got the drop on Lee just after you left," Coldhammer said. "Then they surprised me." He looked sour. "Everyone else was kind of worried about tryin' anything . . ." He was not really criticizing the men, just noting the facts.

"We all had pooled some of our money back in Missouri. The idea was to have enough stake for all when we got to Oregon. Pepperdine and his men took the box. They grabbed Miz Wright and Miss Erline, took some horses, and rode off."

"Why didn't you send someone for me as soon as they were gone?" Calhoun asked harshly.

"They scattered the goddamn horses is why," Lije Wilkins snarled. His gray whiskers shook with anger.

Coldhammer nodded. "We had us a time tryin' to round 'em up. By then, I figured you were too far off, and I knew we had to get movin'."

Calhoun nodded. It made sense.

"Well, when do we leave?" Lee Wilkins demanded.

"I'm leavin' at first light," Calhoun said. He knew it would be foolhardy to leave now. "You ain't leavin' at all."

"Like hell I ain't," Wilkins snapped. His eyes were wild.

"Shut your mouth, boy," his father growled at him.

"No, Pa. I aim to go." He flushed. "I got to see that Miss Erline is all right."

"This ain't no church picnic, boy," Gus Stewart said.

"That's right," Coldhammer said, mostly calmly. "I know you're fond of Miss Erline, boy, but you can't do nothin' here."

"Goddamnit, yes I can," Wilkins insisted.

"Listen to me, boy," Coldhammer said coldly. "This ain't a matter of runnin' down some petty criminal. This here is huntin' down five hard-pressed and desperate men and killin' 'em. In cold blood like as not."

He paused for a breath. "You know there ain't no law out here but what we make ourselves. All the things those bastards did—defilin' women, snatchin' folks, stealin' horses, and all the rest—are hangin' offenses back in the States. Mister Calhoun is the executioner. You ain't up to it."

Coldhammer had sounded as if he was trying to convince himself as well as the others.

"But what about the money, damnit?" Charlie Borgum asked.

The other men nodded in agreement. They had all been wondering and knew someone had to ask.

"What about it?" Coldhammer responded. He knew what they were thinking; had thought it himself.

"What's to stop Calhoun there from just runnin' off with the money?" Borgum said. "Our money. Hell, maybe he's even in on it."

The murmur of acknowledgment stopped quickly when Calhoun said with quiet deadliness, "I've killed men for lesser insults, Mister Borgum."

Borgum's mouth flapped, and fear grew in his eyes. "I didn't mean . . . I—"

"Shut up, Charlie," Coldhammer snapped. "How can you think he's one of them when he killed one?"

"Maybe they had a fallin' out," Lee Wilkins interjected. "Folks—especially those on the wrong side of the law—do more often than not."

"You've had a heap of experience with such men, have you?" Coldhammer demanded.

"Well, no, but—"

"Then button your lip." Coldhammer paused, glowering at the other men. "I trust Mister Calhoun. I trust that he'll find those bastards, visit justice on them, and then bring back the two women—and the money."

He knew he was taking a risk, but he felt it necessary. He didn't really suspect Calhoun was connected with those men. However, that did not necessarily mean he might not try something. He could just take the money and keep riding.

If that happened, there was nothing he could do. He had to take the chance.

"We'll be up shit creek without that cash, Cap'n," Stewart said quietly.

"We're without that money now, Gus," Coldhammer said rationally.

"We could insist that Lee go with him," Borgum offered, trying not to offend.

"What do you think his chances are of gettin' back here alive?" Coldhammer asked, his voice cold again.

"Not very good," Borgum said with resignation.

"Besides," Coldhammer pressed, "we're gonna need all the guns we got if we get attacked by Injuns again."

The other men muttered, but they knew they were helpless. They had to put their faith in Calhoun.

"Well, Mister Calhoun, what do we do now?" Coldhammer asked.

Calhoun drew a rough map in the dirt. "You follow this way. The trail's fairly well marked by those who've gone before. I figure you ought to make Fort Hall in less than two weeks. Ten days if you push it some."

"And you?"

Calhoun fired up a cigarette. "I'll leave early. Try to pick up their trail. After that . . ." He shrugged. Who could say what would happen out in that vast wilderness?

"Where're you gonna meet us?" Lee Wilkins asked. His tone was tight. He wanted to go along, though he knew that would be incredibly foolish.

"Hell if I know," Calhoun snapped. He was tired of all this talk; all the subtle and not so subtle accusations.

He regained his control. "Depends on how long it takes me to find those sons a bitches. Could be a day or two, and I'll catch you before Fort Hall. Could be a couple of weeks and you'll be almost in Oregon."

He paused to take a deep swallow of whiskey. "If I ain't caught up by Fort Hall, stay there a couple days to rest yourselves and the horses. You might be able to hire another guide there to take you the rest of the way."

The men were not happy, but there was nothing they could say or do. They nodded and drifted off into the rain toward their wagons.

Calhoun spent an uncomfortable night under the Coldhammer wagon. Because of it, he was as irritable as hell come morning. It was not thoughts of Erline Rae that had disturbed his sleep. He didn't love her; nor she him. He was bothered, though, at the feeling of having been played for a fool by Pepperdine and the others.

He finally gave up trying to sleep, though it was still dark. He tossed off his covers, dressed, and moved out under the tarp. He stretched and yawned. Then walked out.

It had stopped raining, though the air was still thick with mist and fog.

After taking care of his personal business, he returned and tossed some chips on the remains of last night's fire. With the flames snapping, he put coffee on. He squatted, rubbing his hands in front of the flames, happy for the warmth.

With a cup of coffee inside him, Calhoun put some bacon on to fry.

Polly came out of the wagon, rubbing her eyes. She had the disheveled look of someone who had just woken, but she looked mighty good to him. She drifted off into the mist and then returned, shivering. She pulled her shawl closer around her shoulders and hunkered down next to Calhoun. Neither said anything for a while.

Finally, Polly asked quietly, "There enough for me?" She pointed to the frying pan.

"I suppose," Calhoun allowed grudgingly.

"How long before it's ready?"

"Long enough," Calhoun said. There was a rough edge of desire in his voice.

Polly jerked her head around and looked at Calhoun in some surprise. Heat flamed inside her at the thought. Then reality began to intrude.

"My folks," Polly said lamely, voice quivering a little.

Calhoun shrugged.

"And all the others." Polly waved a hand around at the silent, drenched camp.

Calhoun shrugged again, unconcerned. At this point he didn't much care what anyone saw him do.

Polly thought for a few moments. But the burning inside of her began to override her reason. She shuffled over and into the warm curl of Calhoun's strong arm.

She snuggled against him, knowing that she could not stay there long. She wanted him, almost desperately, but they had so very little time.

Calhoun rode out of the camp less than half an hour later. He was sated from food and surreptitiously, hastily made love.

After the brief encounter with Polly, he had filled

their plates. Suddenly he wanted to be on the move. Pepperdine and the others had almost a full twenty-four hours head start on him. They would be hard to track after all the rain.

He gulped down spoonfuls of bacon and beans. He slurped coffee.

When he finished, Calhoun allowed Polly to kiss him, and then he hurriedly saddled the horse and culled a mule out of the herd. He was aware that Polly was standing in the drizzle, watching him ride out. He could read nothing on her face.

Polly knew, as she stared at his rapidly departing back, that it would be the last time she would ever be close to Calhoun. She was certain that he would return, but she knew deep in her heart, that he would not ride into her life again. She was filled with sadness. At the same time, however, she felt rather relieved.

The last shocked her a bit, until it dawned on her that she was better off for it all. Better off for having met and dallied with Calhoun; better off for having him out of her life.

Wade Calhoun had taught her much, but she knew that he would never be hers. Not completely. He was not a man who could be roped permanently by any woman.

She turned back to her wagon. Her father and mother were just rising. Polly hurried to the fire, to make it look like she was working. As she knelt, she took one last look over her shoulder. Calhoun was nowhere to be seen.

Calhoun rode southeast, toward their last camp.

Already his thoughts had turned from Polly to Erline Rae. And to the unfortunate Clair Wright. The two women would be having a hard time of it, he figured, knowing Pepperdine and the others.

He pushed the horse a little, a sense of urgency driving him. He might not love Erline Rae; he might barely know Clair, but he was not a man to let women be so abused. He would not be content to let this drop until retribution had been enacted.

Without having to hunt or mark trails or scout in all directions for Indians, he made good time. He was at the old camp before noon. The intermittent drizzle had finally stopped, though the skies remained leaden.

Calhoun stopped and loosened the saddle so the horse could breathe. He hobbled the animals and then searched the area, foot by foot. Despite the heavy rains that had fallen since the kidnappings, there were still indications as to where the miscreants had fled.

As he had suspected, they had headed into the rolling, rocky lands southwest of South Pass. That would make the trailing even harder.

Such things did not daunt Calhoun. He would do what he had to do.

He tightened the saddle. As he pulled himself onto his horse, Calhoun wondered why he was doing this. There was nothing in it for him. Nothing, that is, he finally admitted to himself, but a sense of justice accomplished. That was enough at times.

Calhoun pressed throughout the day. He figured that with five men, two women, and several pack mules, the group would be slowed. He should have been able to make better time, seeing as how he was alone and with only one pack animal. However, having to track the group would slow him.

He also knew that Pepperdine would not be the kind of man to go easy on friend, animal, or woman. Pepperdine would push them to the brink of death before he gave them a break.

Calhoun finally called it quits for the day just after dark. He could not follow a trail in the night. He was weary by the time he had picked out a campsite for himself. The lack of sleep the night before, the long days in the saddle, and the twenty-four hours of steady, cold rain all served to tire him.

Within an hour, he had a fire going and had eaten. After a last cigarette, he spread out his bedroll and crawled into it. He was asleep almost instantly.

CHAPTER

* 22 *

With all the tracking he had to do, it took Calhoun more than four days to reach Jim Bridger's Fort. The last time he had been there, the old mountain man himself had been in residence and spun his tales. Calhoun had enjoyed that as much as anything these past several years.

He wondered if it would be the same now, though. He had heard rumors that the Latter-day Saints, Mormons as they were known to outsiders, had been feuding with Bridger.

It wasn't. Calhoun noticed that right off when he rode through the sagging picket walls and into the shabby assortment of old wood buildings. Where once there were former mountain men, many still clad in buckskins, often with a jug of Taos Lightning in hand, there now were hard-eyed, solemn Mormons.

Calhoun was not fond of these pious, overbearing people. They had strange ways about them, from what little Calhoun had seen of them. On the other hand, they had never really bothered him. They were just different, was all, and he tended to avoid them if he could.

A man who was dressed better than the others stepped out of one building and watched Calhoun's slow progress. The man looked officious. Deciding the man was as good a place as any to start looking for information, Calhoun angled in his direction.

Calhoun stopped. Casually he took a good long sip from his canteen. Then he dismounted. He pulled fixings from his pocket and rolled a cigarette.

"You in charge here?" Calhoun finally asked, squinting through the cloud of smoke.

"I am." The man's voice was deep, resonant. "Hiram Flake at your service, sir." He made no move to shake hands; indeed, he was staring without favor on Calhoun. His bushy gray eyebrows raised in question.

"Wade Calhoun."

"What can I do for you, Mister Calhoun?"

"I'm lookin' for some folks," Calhoun said easily.

"Oh?" Flake was noncommittal.

Calhoun could hear, though, what was not said. "They're not of your people," he offered. He thought he could see Flake relax infinitesimally.

"They are Gentiles?"

"If that's what you call folks not of your religious leanings." When Flake nodded, Calhoun said, "There was seven of 'em. Five men and two women."

Flake made a face like he had no knowledge of any of this.

"One's a big bear of a man. Another's a short,

very fat feller. Another's a little son of a . . . a teeny little feller. Laughs like he's more than half *loco.*"

"They aren't here."

"They been here recent?"

Flake said nothing for some moments. He looked blandly at Calhoun, who puffed quietly.

Calhoun had heard some shuffling behind him and he nonchalantly dropped his right hand so it rested near the butt of a Dragoon.

"Why do you want them?" Flake finally asked.

"Personal business to discuss with 'em."

Flake went into his dull stare again. Then the light came back on in his eyes. "They were here."

"When?"

"Two days. Three." Flake shrugged.

Calhoun dropped the smoldering cigarette butt and crushed it under foot. "Mister Flake," he said harshly, "you don't play the fool very well."

Flake started, anger flickering in his eyes. "I don't take kindly to insults, sir." His voice was rough and raspy.

"You don't strike me as a stupid man, Mister Flake. I don't figure you really expect me to believe you don't know when five unknown men—accompanied by two attractive young women—come riding through your place here. Do you?" His eyes were hard.

Flake almost smiled. "They were here for several hours two days ago."

"Only several hours?" Calhoun managed to hide his surprise. With all the wagon trains that passed through here on the way to California, he had figured that Pepperdine and the others would spend at least a day to rest the horses. Perhaps, he thought, they decided that to spend a day with such overtly pious folk as the Mormons would not really be a rest.

"That's all."

"Then they just rode out?"

"Yessir."

"Which way?"

"I wasn't payin' much mind, you understand, but they were seen heading mostly south and west."

"All of them went?" Calhoun still found such a thing hard to believe.

Flake hesitated, and Calhoun knew right away that there was more to it than the Mormon leader was saying.

Flake knew that Calhoun was aware of it, too, and he silently rebuked himself for his mistake. "All but one," he finally admitted.

"Who?"

"He gave his name as Dillard."

Calhoun nodded. "Scaredy seemin' feller?"

"Yes." Flake paused, then asked, "Just what is your business with these people, Mister Calhoun?"

Calhoun was hardly listening. He was wondering why Chuck Dillard had not gone with the others. He also wanted to know where Dillard was. Flake's words finally filtered through, though.

"They took some things didn't belong to 'em," Calhoun said. He didn't want to say more. Nor had he lied.

"That seems to be a trait with them."

"What?" Calhoun asked, startled but covering it after a moment.

"This Dillard's being held for theft."

"What'd he take?"

"Some supplies from our store. Walked out without paying." Flake sounded deeply offended.

Calhoun unconsciously chewed his lower lip while he thought. He was not sure how far he could go with Flake, or with these Mormon people. He decided to test the waters.

"I don't reckon you'd like to hand him over to me," Calhoun said evenly.

"That would be highly irregular."

"I suppose it would."

"Why would I do something like that?"

"What's he going to get here?" Calhoun countered. "For stealin' some supplies? Unless he stole one heap of goods."

"Not many," Flake admitted.

"I want him for crimes a lot worse than stealin' a few beans." He paused, then decided to push ahead. "Was he to be released to me, he'd pay full price."

"Afraid I can't do that, Mister Calhoun," Flake said after a momentary hesitation. "We have laws and such." He cast his eyes toward the heavens.

Calhoun nodded. "I understand." He sighed. "You have someplace I can line my flue before I set out after those others?" He patted his stomach.

Flake pointed.

"Obliged." Calhoun walked toward the indicated building, towing the skewbald behind him.

The service was adequate; the food excellent.

Finally he pushed himself up and walked outside. The sun was dipping and a few clouds were blowing in. He expected no rain from the clouds. He walked across the compound to Flake's office and knocked.

When he received permission to enter, he did. He could tell nothing on Flake's face.

"I was wonderin' if there'd be trouble with me stayin' the night here, Mister Flake."

"I see no reason such a thing'd cause trouble, Mister Calhoun."

Calhoun nodded. "There a place for me?"

"We have a barracks-type room where single men, those not with a wagon train, stay."

"Point the way."

Flake did. He also showed Calhoun where the livery was.

Calhoun walked the horse to the livery and unsaddled it. He was not about to leave the fancy Mexican-style saddle in the livery. He carted it, his bedroll and saddlebags to his quarters.

He picked out a bunk and put his gear on it. Then he walked to a window. Rolling a cigarette, he puffed while he stood there and looked out.

His vigilance was finally rewarded. He saw a man carrying a towel-covered tray. The man entered a log building to Calhoun's left. A few minutes later he came back out accompanied by a man wearing a badge. They headed toward the restaurant.

With a growing feeling of certainty at what needed to be done, Calhoun turned and went to his bunk. He lay on his back, thankful that he was the room's only occupant. Pulling his hat over his eyes, he dozed off.

When he awoke, he headed for the outhouse around back. On the way back to the bunkhouse, he checked the moon, which played peek-a-boo with the clouds. It was about midnight, he estimated. His internal clock had not failed him.

He grabbed his few things and walked silently to the livery. He saddled his horse and patted the animal's neck. Then he packed the mule. He walked to the stable door and looked out. Seeing no one, he went outside, towing the animals.

He kept to the line of buildings, heading toward what he believed to be the jail. It was next to Flake's office.

Calhoun slipped into the alley next to the jail. Leaving the beasts, he tested the door. It was locked, but the bolt seemed flimsy.

Calhoun grabbed the door handle with his right hand. Then he jerked his shoulder, punching the door with it. The lock cracked away from the jamb. It sounded loud in the still night, and Calhoun froze.

He gave it a minute, but no one seemed to pay any heed. Calhoun shoved the door open and stepped inside. There were no windows in the front or side, and he spotted only one in the back, by the cells. He lit a lantern, keeping it low.

With a few minutes of searching the desk, he found a ring of keys. With the lantern in one hand and the keys in the other, he headed toward the three small cells crammed into the back of the office. They had the look of impermanence. Two were empty. Chuck Dillard occupied the third.

Dillard had been woken with the noise of the door breaking. Now he sat almost trembling in fear as he waited whatever was coming. His eyes bugged when he saw Calhoun.

"Shit," he breathed.

Dillard seemed scared witless. It was a wonder that he would've had the nerve to steal anything outright, like he had been accused of doing. A glint of hope flickered in his eyes. "You come to get me out, didn't you?" he asked. He appeared to be on the verge of tears.

"Not exactly." Calhoun set the lantern down and unlocked the door. With the light flickering on the dull wood walls, Calhoun pulled his Bowie knife from the shoulder sheath that dangled under his left armpit and entered the cell.

"You and your cronies've caused many folks a heap of grief," Calhoun said in deadly tones. "Now's the time for you to meet justice."

"What in the hell're you talkin' about?" Dillard stammered. "I wasn't . . . I didn't . . ."

"Christ, boy, have some gumption for once in your life," Calhoun snapped in annoyance.

Dillard was still babbling with fear when Calhoun finished him off with the Bowie.

Calhoun wiped the knife blade clean on Dillard's shirt and slipped it back into the sheath. He went out, locked the cell, and brought the lantern back to the desk. He turned it off and left by the side door.

Swiftly he walked his horse and mule toward the

gate. It was ajar, which it hadn't been before. Calhoun nodded. He mounted the horse and rode out of the fort. As soon as he was outside the log walls, he kicked the horse into a gallop.

CHAPTER

* 23 *

Calhoun instinctively headed southwest. He knew that the only thing between Fort Bridger and California were the Mormon settlements clustered on the southeastern shores of the Great Salt Lake. He also knew there was nothing south of Fort Bridger except hostile Indians and mean mountains, until one reached Santa Fe.

Shortly before noon, Calhoun found Pepperdine's trail. It took some searching, but he finally managed to pick out the right track from the maze left by thousands of wagons, horses, mules, and oxen.

With more surety, he picked up the pace, even though he was into the mountains now. Only once in a while did he stop and check to make sure he was still on the right trail. It was with some dismay that he could not locate it late in the day.

Growing more agitated with each passing minute, he rode back and forth across the wide, beaten-down California Trail. Still, he found nothing.

"Shit," Calhoun muttered.

Angrily he swung around and rode hard, dragging the reluctant pack mule behind him. He went almost to the spot where he had last checked the trail. He stopped and searched again.

He was relieved when he found it. More slowly, he headed west again. Being in the mountains, it was harder to follow the trail. But he kept at it, moving slowly.

Several miles on, he stopped and sat, irritated at himself for not having seen it before. The trail had spun more southward, through a gap in the mountains.

Shedding the self-annoyance, he picked up the pace again. Eventually Pepperdine's trail turned toward the southwest again.

Calhoun rode until well after dark. He finally pulled up in a wooded little canyon. A slip of a stream tumbled down over the rocks and bubbled frothily through the brush and trees.

Calhoun had neither the time nor inclination to enjoy it. He simply made a quick camp, heated some buffalo and coffee, ate, and turned in.

After a quick breakfast of bacon and coffee, Calhoun hit the trail again. It was barely light. He checked just after starting, to make sure he was still on Pepperdine's trail, a little worried that he might have lost it in the darkness the night before.

He spotted it right off, giving thanks again that two of the horses had at least one odd shoe each.

Slowed by the mountains, it was almost four days before he was in the vicinity of the towns that were spread out from the Mormon capital of Salt Lake City.

The trail, though, did not go into any of those towns; nor had it followed the California Trail very closely. He found that odd, and he wondered about it.

Calhoun was running low on supplies, and he silently cursed himself for not having stocked up in Fort Bridger. Since he hadn't, he left Pepperdine's track and pulled into the first Mormon town he found.

He was not greeted with much warmth. This was a town that saw few of the travelers on their way to California, or any other Gentiles. They were not very friendly toward Calhoun. Not that they were antagonistic. They spoke mildly and served him quickly and with efficiency. It was evident, though, that they had no liking for him and that they did not want to see him to linger.

He had no plans to anyway, and so was riding back out of town as soon as the mule was packed.

The short detour did help explain why Pepperdine's track veered off. It also gave Calhoun an indication of just where Pepperdine and the others were headed.

It had suddenly dawned on Calhoun that after the trouble Pepperdine and the others had had in Fort Bridger, they would not be in a hurry to get mixed up with any other Mormons. Therefore, they were giving the Mormon settlements a wide berth.

Calhoun also figured that they would be fixing to head almost due west once they got past the settlements and meet up with the California Trail way out beyond the Great Salt Lake.

He hurried along with a feeling of both dread and expectation. He had been that way before; had faced that mean, deadly stretch of salt desert. It was a man killer, he knew. He wondered if Pepperdine or any of those with him knew it. If they didn't, they would be in bad trouble, and Calhoun should be able to catch them soon. Calhoun figured he was not far behind them anyway.

If they did know, they were probably prepared, and that would make Calhoun's job all the harder. It would also, though, give the women a better chance of survival.

Calhoun swung off once more and into another town. He suspected it was the last one he might find. Again he was not greeted very hospitably, but he ignored that.

He bought six canteens and several sacks of horse grain. Just before leaving the small store, he also impulsively bought a new hat. He threw his old one on the floor as he put the new on.

Outside, he filled the new canteens and hung them and the grain on the mule. He also filled his old canteen and returned that to its usual position of dangling from his saddle horn.

Then he was on his way once again.

He stopped early in the afternoon, figuring it wise to give the horse and mule a break before heading into the heart of the salt desert.

The resting spot was not the best he ever had, but better than some. He went sparingly on his water, and husbanded his sparse supply of fuel as he ate. He tended the horses and then turned in. It was barely past noon.

Calhoun remembered the salt desert as a bizarre place, and he did not look forward to passing through it again. The hot, bright summer sun would beat down on the flat, barren expanse, and bounce back off the gleaming whiteness of the sand. It would hurt the eyes, dry the mouth, and fool the mind, if one let it.

That was why he headed into it soon after dusk. He had slept for several hours, then rose and made another meal. He made sure the horse and mule ate a fair portion of grain.

After he ate, he saddled the horse, packed the mule, kicked sand over the fire, and headed out.

Calhoun rode through the night, grateful for its coolness. Just after dawn, he stopped. There was no cover to be seen, so he just pulled up when he had had enough of the glare and the rising heat.

He unsaddled the horse and unpacked the mule. It was tedious, hot work, but necessary, and by the time he finished, he was coated with sweat.

He poured water from a canteen into his hat and held it for the horse to drink from. Then he did the same for the mule. After brushing both animals down, he filled feed bags and hung one over each animal's muzzle.

Finally he was able to see to his own needs. After relieving himself, he rinsed off his head and hands with water. He pounded picket pins into the ground and tied the animals to them.

At last he rigged up a sort of tent for himself from his bedroll and a couple of sticks he had brought along. He crawled inside it and slept.

He spent two more days and nights the same way, traveling in the darkness, sleeping during the inferno of daylight. Then he began to see signs that he was nearing the end of the desert. The land began sloping upward toward more mountains, though these were not heavily wooded ones, and a little grass and sage began appearing.

Calhoun was relieved. He was running low on water, though he had been trying to use it sparingly. He was also tired of eating jerky and not having coffee because there was no fuel for fires.

He had occasionally seen the distinctive track of the two horses with Pepperdine's bunch, so he knew he was still on the right trail. He was only a little surprised that he had not seen Pepperdine or one of the others dead; or had not come upon them. He was certain now that at least one of them had been this way before and knew what he was doing.

The desert did not end abruptly; it just sort of petered out as the land rose into rocky, barren mountains. He pressed on, looking more now for a source of water than for Pepperdine's trail.

He knew there were streams around, but finding one often could be tricky. At this time of year, many, if not most, of the streams and springs were dried up.

Calhoun finally found a reasonable-looking spot in a valley, though he had had to come a lot farther than he had planned on. He pulled up in some brush and small cottonwoods and sycamores. A trickle of water plodded along. He thought it was Nelson Creek, but he was not sure.

There was not a lot of water in the stream, but it was far better than nothing. With the shade of the brush, trees, and surrounding gray cliffs, it was downright pleasant after the inferno of the salt desert.

It was late in the day, and Calhoun was exhausted. He had continued traveling at night, and then as he worked into higher country, kept going even after daylight.

Wearily he unsaddled the horse and dropped the saddle and small, sweat-soaked blanket under a tree. Then he pulled his small stash of supplies off the mule and stacked them near the saddle.

At times like this, Calhoun hated taking care of animals; but he also knew that it was these times when they most needed it. So he did the chores. Only after he had finished with the beasts did he see to his own needs.

He was stiff and sore the next morning. He was still tired, too. With a sigh of weariness, he checked the horse and mule. Both looked in fairly good shape, but Calhoun suddenly decided that the animals needed more rest.

It wouldn't hurt him any, either, he knew, but that was not what had swayed him.

Should either animal go under, Calhoun would be in bad shape. On foot or without supplies, he would have little chance of saving Erline Rae and Clair Wright. He would survive, he had no doubt, but he would have no chance of catching Pepperdine before the outlaw and his cronies made it to California, whether in the company of a wagon train or on their own.

He had no regrets about deciding that he would

stay here at least through the night and the day. That would give Pepperdine and the others time to put more distance between themselves and Calhoun. He figured it was worth it, though. With the horse rested and well fed, he could make better time tomorrow.

He pushed it when he finally took up the trail again. Though the altitude was fairly high, the land was mostly flat and barren. Sage, short, yellowed grass, and some odd, whitish bushes dotted the bleak country.

Calhoun paid more attention to Pepperdine's tracks again, but he had no trouble following them. No one had been by this way in ages, other than Pepperdine's group. That much was evident.

Other than two small bands of Indians he had spotted far off, Calhoun had seen no one. He was not sure what kind of Indians they were, but even at a distance he saw they were not mounted, and so presented no danger.

He spent a long day on the trail before finally calling it a night. He camped in the open, using sage for a fire to cook a meal. Sage also fed the horses, since he was almost out of grain. His canteens were full, though, and that made a big difference.

As he climbed into his bedroll, he suddenly had the feeling that he was close to his quarry. He didn't know how, but his hunches had always been right before, and he had learned to accept them.

After a filling breakfast in the morning, he hit the trail. Something seemed to be pushing him, and he gave in to the feeling.

Around noon, he spied a small town off on the horizon. It didn't look promising from this distance, but the tracks seemed to be heading for it. After a while, he began thinking the town was a mirage. The sun was fierce, and he was not at all sure it wasn't playing tricks on him.

Eventually, though, he rode past a dilapidated shack, then several others. He was in the town, though now he decided it was more of a settlement than a real town. It seemed pretty much deserted.

The wind groaned, not fiercely but with a steady, low keening. It made loose boards flap and building walls creak.

Calhoun spotted a few people peering out from behind curtains. There was no one on the streets, if that's what they could be called, though. About halfway through the town, he saw a familiar face. With grim determination stamped on his pitted countenance, he slowly headed that way.

CHAPTER

* 24 *

Calhoun stopped the skewbald horse and dismounted. The scratching of a slightly out of tune violin mingled with the whine of a concertina from inside the building in front of Calhoun.

There was no hitching post, so Calhoun just dropped the reins. He and the horse had been together long enough now, Calhoun figured, that it should stay put. Having the mule tied to the saddle horn would help.

Calhoun took three steps and stopped, facing Bass Cutler.

Cutler was sitting on a short wooden bench with one arm around Erline Rae's shoulders. The woman looked half sick, half resigned as she sat rigidly while Cutler pawed her with his other hand. Cutler's face was red and puffy; his breathing was labored.

"Afternoon, ma'am," Calhoun said calmly. Though the remark was addressed to Erline Rae, Calhoun was looking directly at Cutler.

"Afternoon," Erline Rae said. Her face was pasty in the sunlight. Hope had bloomed in her breast, though.

"What the hell do you want here, Calhoun?" Cutler growled.

He was scared down to his holey socks, but was trying to put on a brave front. He figured that with the others just inside, Calhoun couldn't do too much. Still, Calhoun was crazy enough to not care too much.

"I come to take Miss Erline back. Miz Wright, too." Calhoun's voice had taken on a harder edge.

"She's busy. So's the other'n."

Calhoun was plain sick to death of Bass Cutler, Rollie Pepperdine, and the rest of that bunch. He moved directly in front of Cutler and bent so he could shove his face within inches of the fat man's countenance.

"Unless you'd like me to rip off that arm of yours and beat you to death with it, I'd suggest you move it. Now."

Cutler gulped as he stared into the flat, deadly eyes. He knew he was a dead man if he didn't move—and fast. He dropped his arm, still looking fearfully at Calhoun.

Erline Rae slid off the bench and scuttled a few feet to the side, away from the door.

"Get up," Calhoun ordered.

Cutler ponderously pushed up, sucking in his breath fearfully. "What . . . What're you gonna do wif me?" Cutler asked, voice shaking.

"Same as I did to Dillard."

"You couldn't of done nothin' to Chuck," Cutler blathered. "He's locked up back in that dinky-ass little town . . ." He sputtered to a stop when he saw the devilish grin on Calhoun's face.

"Bein' in that jail didn't give him no room to run," Calhoun said easily.

Cutler swallowed hard, hoping it would force his heart back down out of his throat, where it had become lodged when Calhoun rode up.

"What'd you do to him?" Cutler asked, voice cracking with fear.

"Carved him like a Christmas goose."

Cutler knew he had to do something. His hand flew toward the pistol stuck in his belt.

Calhoun did not even have to step up. From where he was, he snapped an elbow up and out. It caught Cutler in the philtrum, that small concavity between the nose and upper lip.

Cutler's head jerked back, banging on the wall of the building. His hand drooped slackly to his side, and his eyes took a few moments to focus.

Calhoun pulled Cutler's revolver free and tossed it off into the street behind him. "Just so you won't be tempted again," Calhoun said quietly.

After what Cutler, Pepperdine, and the others had done to Erline Rae and, Calhoun assumed, Clair Wright, Calhoun almost enjoyed the terror in Cutler's eyes. He saw it as a fitting thing, considering.

Calhoun pulled his Bowie knife. "Now," he said slowly, letting the surety of his words come through, "supposin' you just tell me where the others are. And," he added after a moment's pause, "where the money is."

"The others're inside," Cutler answered hastily, hoping to stave off what was seemingly inevitable. "Havin' themselves a whoop-up."

"Why ain't you in there with 'em?"

"Takin' a break for a spell." Cutler tried to smile but failed. "I ain't as spry as I used to be, so I thought I'd set a spell."

"And Pepperdine let you take Miss Erline out here?" Calhoun was almost incredulous.

"They got tired of me," Erline Rae said. She wasn't sure how she felt about that. On the one hand, she was mostly relieved that for even just a short time she had to contend only with Bass Cutler. On the other hand, it was a blow to her to know that she was now considered so old hat as to not be wanted any longer, even by those animals.

"They found others?" Calhoun asked harshly. Again, he was talking to Erline Rae, but looking at Cutler.

"Two," Cutler admitted.

"Who?" Calhoun asked. He looked at Erline Rae, no longer worried about Cutler. He was rather surprised, wondering where they had come across other women out here on the far edge of nowhere.

"Best we can figure it," Erline Rae said, her voice losing some of its fear and resignation, "this place was settled by Mormons. From what we heard, they had wanted to try to minister to the Indians in these parts."

She paused, licking her dry lips. She felt as if she had not had enough water in weeks. "Anyway, after some Indian trouble up north, folks from most of the towns like these were called home."

Erline Rae shrugged diffidently. "I guess some travelers got off the trail one day and wandered and wandered till they got here. They just stayed. There's just a few of them, less than a dozen, I guess. Three women, one of them about Miz Wilkins's age."

"So Pepperdine and the others just come in here and took them two women?" He thought it amazing that any man would let that happen without putting up some kind of fight.

"The menfolk protested, but Rollie killed one and Tiny killed another. We ain't seen most of the others since."

Calhoun nodded. That made a little more sense. He turned back to Cutler. "Now, where's the money?"

Cutler cursed to himself, but he did not let his anger show. He thought that with all the other talk that Calhoun might forget about the money. "Don't know," he mumbled.

Calhoun calmly placed the sharp tip of the Bowie's blade on Cutler's left cheekbone. Then he slowly drew it downward, leaving behind a thin cut that seeped blood.

When the blade fell off Cutler's jaw, Calhoun said, "I can continue, if you fancy that."

"In there." Cutler carefully jerked a thumb over his shoulder, indicating the building. "Rollie keeps the box with him most all the time. If he ain't with it, Tiny is."

Calhoun accepted it calmly and looked to Erline Rae for confirmation.

Cutler breathed in relief. He was beginning to think he would make it through all this. He had cooperated, told Calhoun all he wanted to know.

Erline Rae nodded once.

Calhoun turned cold eyes on Bass Cutler. He could see no reason for the fat man to go on living. Cutler had raped and robbed, probably killed, across a number of states and territories. The world would be a better place without him, Calhoun figured.

Cutler was still trying to regain his confidence when the large blade of the Bowie slid into his guts like raw meat into a wolf. So smooth was it, that it took some moments for Cutler to realize it.

"Jesus!" Cutler breathed. He looked down, saw the knife into his belly up to the hilt, and then looked back into Calhoun's eyes. "Why?" he asked. He winced as the pain spread throughout him.

Calhoun shrugged. "'Cause you're a festerin' little puke," he said easily. "And it's high time your misdeeds brought you justice."

Cutler's knees were wobbly as his lifeblood flowed out over Calhoun's hand and knife. His eyes were having a little trouble focusing.

Calhoun stepped back, pulling the knife free as he did. He wiped it on Cutler's shirt and then slid it back into the sheath. He wiped his hand off.

Cutler stood there a few moments more, still disbelieving. Then he sank to his knees. He continued to glance between the blood-welling hole in his stomach and Calhoun's eyes.

After what seemed to be ages to Erline Rae, Cutler fell. His nose broke when he hit the dirt, but he did not know it. He was dead.

Calhoun looked down at Cutler for a moment. He held no remorse for what he had done. Cutler had gotten only what he deserved. Calhoun moved to

Erline Rae's side. "You all right?" he asked.

Erline Rae nodded. She smiled at him. "Thank you," she breathed. She looked more animated now that Cutler was dead and Calhoun was here.

Calhoun shrugged. "All the others inside?" he asked.

"Yep."

"There a back door? Side window?"

"Nope." Erline Rae pointed to the door. "This's the only way in or out."

Calhoun stood there thinking. He was tired of all this and wanted it to be over as quickly as possible. These men had committed far too much mayhem. Calhoun regretted not having taken care of this when he had the first run-in with Rollie Pepperdine. He hadn't, though. A few people had died, and several others had suffered tremendously as a result.

As Calhoun figured it, he had two alternatives: Just walk on into the building and see what he could do; or he could try to get them out here.

His sense of perversity and daring favored the former, though that was the more foolish choice. He did not know the layout of the building, nor where the people were positioned. He figured two of the townsfolk were playing the instruments, and there also were the two women besides Clair. They could get hurt if Calhoun just wandered in and started pumping out lead.

The latter was more reasonable in most ways, but that also presented a problem: Getting Pepperdine and the three others out here. If he opened the door and shouted for them, the outlaws just might come out using townsfolk as shields.

He looked at Erline Rae, who was staring at him in eager expectation. He could use her, but that did not set well with him.

He also supposed he could sit here and wait till one or more of the owlhoots wondered where Cutler and Erline Rae were and came out to look. He could take them one at a time that way. That, however, was chancy.

"How many rooms in there?" he asked.

"Two," Erline Rae answered, looking at him in question. "Big, mostly empty room out front here. They've been usin' it as a saloon and dance hall since we got here yesterday. The other's a small room off the back. That's where they . . ."

"No need to say more," Calhoun said quietly. It made his flesh crawl to know that women were being so ill-used.

The information did not help him, though. At any one time, one of the outlaws might be in the back room. If he burst in the front, he would endanger not only himself but any of the captives.

He growled low in his throat, angry at knowing he had no choice but to have Erline Rae help. Nothing could be done about it, and wasting time would not further their cause.

"You want to get out of here, you'll have to help out."

"I'll do anything!" Erline Rae said fervently. She meant it, too.

Erline Rae North was no fool. She knew her life

would not be easy even if she got away from Pepperdine. She even knew she had no hope of a future with Calhoun. However, she realized that she would be better off almost anywhere than with this band of beasts, and that she might have an easy time of finding a husband and settling down if she got to Oregon.

"Go on in there and tell one of them boys to come out here."

"Which one?" Eagerness crept into her voice.

"Don't matter. Whoever's nearest the door."

"You just want me to tell him you're out here waitin' for him?" she asked, plainly skeptical that such a thing would work.

"Too risky. You do that, he'll holler for the others. Then they'll most likely put you and all those others under the gun before they come out."

That gave Erline Rae pause. She had no idea of what else to do, but what Calhoun had said made sense.

"Just go in there and tell him that after Cutler dragged you outside here, something happened to him. He's sick or somethin' and that he needs help. That ought to bring one of 'em. Leave the rest to me."

Erline Rae smiled. It was not one of pleasure. These men had abused her for years, most of the time with her father's willing support. Now it was time they were paid back. She aimed to see these men dead.

She turned. Gripping the door handle, she paused to collect herself. She didn't want to walk in grinning like a cat. They would know something was wrong, considering how she had been since she had been taken from the wagon train. With a solemn face, she pushed the door open and walked in.

CHAPTER

✴ 25 ✴

Erline Rae North was used to acting; she had had to do it all her short life. She had had to seem pleased with the men her father had forced on her. Had to pretend to like those men when she was with them, making them feel big and important. Had to lie when the law snooped around their cabin back in Missouri. This was nothing new to her.

Billy Quince was closest to the door. He had a bottle of whiskey in hand. The liquor had dulled his usually bright eyes and made his handsome face slack. Erline Rae was surprised to see him alone, until she noticed that the townswoman with whom he had taken up was working by the stove.

When her father had first brought Quince around, she thought him nice looking. He was neat and well-cared for. She had felt relief, figuring that Quince would know how to treat a woman.

She had been so utterly wrong in that belief. Quince turned out to be one of the worst beasts she had ever been with. He had a nasty disposition and a propensity for finding pleasure in giving pain to women. Erline Rae was glad he was nearest, and would get his just rewards first.

She sidled up to him and tugged on his sleeve.

"Billy," she said meekly, looking frightened and worried. "Billy, somethin's gone wrong with Bass."

"So?" Quince had no liking for anyone, least of all blubbery Bass Cutler.

"Come on and see," Erline Rae said plaintively.

"What for?"

"Come on, Billy," Erline Rae whined. Her voice had little-girl tones to it. "He took me outside"—she looked down in embarrassment—"you know."

Quince grinned. It made him look like an innocent boy, masking his real nature. "So, the fat old bastard wasn't satisfied with usin' the back room like everyone else, eh?" He laughed. "Well, that's got nothin' to do with me."

"He's took sick or somethin', and I'm concerned for him."

"Took sick?"

"Yeah. He just got this funny look on his face and then keeled over. I think he's gonna pass over to the beyond."

Quince laughed. "Serves the fat bastard right."

Erline Rae veered slightly off tack. "Rollie's fond of him, you know."

"So?" Quince was indifferent.

"It turns out Bass died 'cause you wouldn't come help, and Rollie finds out about it . . ." She let the words trail off. There was no need to finish.

"All right, damnit," Quince snapped. He pushed off the wall, irritated. With the bottle swinging in one hand, he followed Erline Rae outside.

A relaxed Calhoun was waiting just beside the door.

He heard Erline Rae say, "He's right out here, by the bench . . ."

The woman appeared and stepped to the side. She knew where Calhoun had planned to wait, and she neatly moved to the other side.

As Quince walked out and turned, his back was to Calhoun.

Calhoun's left hand snaked out. He flipped Quince's hat off, toward the front, and then grabbed a fistful of greasy hair. Calhoun jerked Quince's head back. The Bowie knife came up in Calhoun's other hand, heading for the arteries throbbing in Quince's throat.

Quince seemed about to yell, and, even as drunk as he was, he looked like he was not going to give up without a fight. So Erline Rae stepped forward and kicked him viciously between the legs. She felt something akin to satisfaction as she saw Quince sag and his face go pasty.

The blade moved swiftly and a gaping rift appeared in the flesh of Quince's throat. Blood spurted, and Erline Rae had to dance away a few steps to avoid being splattered by it.

Calhoun gave Quince's head a shove and let go of the hair. Quince pitched forward, dead but not quite knowing it. Quince landed in a pile, most of him lying across the lower half of Cutler's body.

"What now?" Erline Rae asked as Calhoun knelt to clean his knife.

He stood and looked at her. There was a look of almost fevered eagerness in the woman's eyes.

"Reckon we ought to finish things up," he offered.

"How?"

Though Calhoun had beaten the stuffing out of Rollie Pepperdine on several occasions, he did not hold the big man lightly. He also knew that Tiny Bates was more than half crazy, which made him dangerous.

Calhoun decided he wanted to get this over with as quickly as possible. The more time he took, the more time there would be for something to go wrong. He didn't care about himself so much, but the lives of others were at stake.

He decided he needed to take Pepperdine and Bates out together. He and Erline Rae would need a different story, though, this time. He called Erline Rae over to him and explained what he wanted.

She nodded solemnly when he had finished. It would be dangerous, she knew, but she didn't care. Not after the life she had lived. To her, it was either get out of that past once and for all, or die.

Once more Erline Rae entered the lion's den.

She headed for Pepperdine, who had Clair on his lap and was slobbering all over her. The top of Clair's calico dress was unbuttoned, but she seemed not to notice, her humiliation was that complete.

Bates stood nearby, pinning one of the townswomen against the wall with his scrawny body. The other captive townswoman was still by the small, cast-iron stove, preparing some food.

Erline Rae cast off her disgust at the tableau and moseyed over to Pepperdine. She had the proper amount of nervousness stamped on her face.

"Bass done with you already?" Pepperdine said, coming up for air long enough to laugh.

"Sort of."

"Eh? What's that supposed to mean?" Pepperdine looked at her sharply, eyes questioning.

"He . . . him and Billy . . . they . . ."

"Well, out with it, woman," Calhoun snapped.

"They got into a tussle." She smiled with shy pride. "Over me." Growing serious again, she said. "Then they pulled their knives. I think they're fixin' to kill each other."

"I don't hear nothin'," Pepperdine said suspiciously.

"The music . . ."

"Knock off that goddamn noise," Pepperdine shouted at the old man and the boy providing the tunes. He threw an empty whiskey bottle at them to emphasize his point.

The racket faded, and Pepperdine sat listening. "I don't hear nothin'."

"Maybe they've already . . ." Erline Rae sounded properly horrified.

"Tiny!" Pepperdine roared. "Come on." He leapt up, dumping Clair unceremoniously on the floor. The unfortunate widow lay there, weeping at all the horrors she had been through in the past couple of weeks.

Bates spun. "What's it?" he asked, blinking stupidly.

But Pepperdine was striding for the door. Before Bates could catch up, Pepperdine suddenly stopped, spun, and walked back. He grabbed Erline Rae's left arm. "I'd be obliged was you to come along, woman," he said.

Erline Rae never knew how she kept the fear off her face when Pepperdine started dragging her across the floor.

"What's goin' on, Rollie?" Bates asked, trying vainly to match Pepperdine's long strides.

"Just shet up and come along."

At the door, Pepperdine stopped momentarily. He grabbed Erline Rae around the throat, yanking her close against him. He pulled a pistol in his other hand. "Get the door, Tiny," he ordered.

Bates giggled in that mad way of his and drew his revolver. Stepping to the side, he jerked the door open.

Pepperdine walked out, moving Erline Rae effortlessly ahead of him.

"See," Erline Rae said, pointing at the two bodies. She did not have to fake her fear this time.

Pepperdine towered over Erline Rae, so his vision was not impeded by his shield. Of course, the woman was less of a shield that he might have desired because of it, too. He looked around, spotted the bodies, a few feet apart to his right. There was nothing untoward in front of him.

Something didn't seem right to Pepperdine, despite the appearance of normalcy. The bodies weren't normal, of course, but that could be explained away easy enough. That was not really what bothered him. What it was, he could not fathom.

He was all set to let Erline Rae loose, but his suspicion stayed him. "Tiny," he called.

Bates, who had stayed just inside the door, responded, "Yeah, Rollie?"

"Come on out here and check these bodies."

Bates eased out the door, pistol held up alongside his right ear. He was cautious. It was why he had stayed inside. He didn't like being out in the open. He glanced around, but saw nothing to worry him. The bodies didn't concern him. There would be more booty to split between two than four.

He slid along the building's wall, then knelt between the two bodies. Without putting his Colt away, he checked each quickly. "Deader'n doornails, the both of 'em," he announced.

"How?"

"Knives."

Pepperdine began to relax.

"Did good jobs on each other, too." Bates giggled crazily. "Hell, Bass managed to cut Billy's throat even after gettin' a shiv in the brisket."

"Does seem they done each other good." Pepperdine began to relax even more, giving Erline Rae some breathing room. Suddenly the import of what Bates had said dawned on him. He tried to tighten his hold on Erline Rae again, swearing softly.

It was too late, though. Erline Rae slid out from under the big arm and skittered into the street. "Wade!" she screamed.

Pepperdine crouched and began swinging toward Erline Rae, bringing his pistol up, cocked.

Bates hesitated, wondering just what was going on.

Calhoun stepped from around the corner of the building, behind Pepperdine. "*Adios,*" Calhoun commented. He fired the double-barreled shotgun once.

Pepperdine bowed backward as the blast ripped his back. He fell to his knees and then onto his face.

Calhoun swung the shotgun at Bates. The small man was no longer kneeling between the bodies. In fact, he was nowhere to be seen.

"Shit," Calhoun muttered. He spun and slid back around the corner. After slipping the shotgun into the scabbard, he climbed onto his saddle. Grabbing the eave of the roof, he pulled himself upward on the strength of his arms. As he got his midsection on the eave, he jerked his legs up and rolled fully onto the roof.

He slipped off his spurs and stuck them in his shirt. Then he stood and drew one of his Dragoons. Crouched, he headed for the back edge of the roof. Near the edge, he went almost flat on his stomach and crept forward until he could peer over the edge. He saw nothing.

He rose and hurried toward where he had started. He got there just in time to see Bates easing around the corner toward the front. If the game he and Bates were playing wasn't so deadly, Calhoun might have thought it humorous. He headed toward the front.

Down below, Bates began to suspect that Calhoun was following him around the building, or at least trying to. He stopped and backed out into the street, stepping over Pepperdine's body along the way. He figured to get a little distance from the building. That way he could cover both sides at the same time. He did move fractionally more to his right than the left, since he knew Calhoun would have to get his horse sooner or later.

"Come on out, Calhoun," he shouted. "Come and show yourself." He let loose a burst of that insane laughter of his.

Calhoun stood up, near the edge of the roof. "Up here, asshole." Calhoun's voice was not loud, but it carried well on the wind.

Bates looked up, startled. He squinted into the sunlight at the dark shadowy figure on the roof. "That you, Calhoun?" he shouted back. He was at a serious disadvantage, what with the sun in his eyes, and the dust blowing up all around him.

"Either drop your piece," he warned. "Or use it."

Bates might be demented, but he had a good instinct for survival. He knew he would have no chance of ever getting away from Calhoun if he gave himself up. Nor would he have any chance of avoiding the noose even if Calhoun brought him back to the wagon train, or to some town somewhere. Better, he figured, to take his chances now.

CHAPTER

✴ 26 ✴

T iny Bates snapped his pistol up and fired. His shot was far off. That was because as his finger was squeezing the trigger, a ball from Calhoun's Dragoon broke his gun arm.

Calhoun's second shot punched a hole in Bates's breast. The third tore through the left eye and out the back of the head.

"Miss Erline," Calhoun called.

"Yes, Mister Calhoun?" The woman's voice floated faintly to Calhoun. Though it came from a little distance, it was strong and unafraid.

"Stay where you are a spell. Till I come for you."

He backed away from the edge and went to the south side of the building, the one opposite his horse and mule. He swung over the side, hung by his hands for a moment, and then dropped to the ground. He headed swiftly toward the front. He figured that if any of the outlaws were still alive, they would expect him from the other direction, where his horse was.

At the corner, he peered around the building. There was no movement. He stepped out and stalked smoothly toward Cutler and Quince. They were the nearest. They also were dead, as Bates had found.

Calhoun then checked Pepperdine. The big man's shirt and back were flayed from the blast of buckshot, but he was still breathing, though barely.

Calhoun peeled the pistol out of Pepperdine's fist and cast it away. He stood, considering for a moment ending Pepperdine's misery. He decided against it, though. Pepperdine would die soon enough anyway, and it would be a waste of powder and lead.

Calhoun felt only a little uneasy as he headed toward Bates. He didn't think Pepperdine had another gun on him, even if he could somehow manage the strength to rise even a little. Still, it was a little unsettling leaving an enemy behind him like that.

As he knelt by Bates, Calhoun made sure he was half turned toward Pepperdine, just in case. Bates was dead, lying in a pool of blood that was rapidly soaking into the dust.

Calhoun rose and surveyed the carnage. He felt no regret for what he had wrought here. Nor did he feel any sense of satisfaction. It was simply something that had to be done, and he had done it with his usual resolve and ruthless efficiency.

"Miss Erline," he called. "You can come on out now."

In a minute, she was at his side, looking around with relief. Her nightmare was over. As they walked toward the building, Erline Rae slipped her arm through Calhoun's, gaining strength from it. Calhoun glanced down, noticing that Pepperdine was dead.

They entered the building. Clair was still lying on

the floor, whimpering. The musicians stood where they had been, looking frightened. The two townswomen were in the same places, too, as if afraid to move.

"Go see to Miz Wright," Calhoun whispered to his companion. As Erline Rae headed toward Clair, Calhoun strolled toward the stove. "That supper ready yet, ma'am?" he asked.

She looked at him, startled into temporary dumbness. To the woman, Calhoun looked like another of those animals who had besieged the town.

"Smells done," Calhoun offered. He tried to smile, but such a thing was always an effort for him.

"Yes," the woman said. The one word squeaked out, having trouble escaping her fear-constricted chest and throat.

"I'd be obliged was you to serve it up for us."

The woman nodded.

Calhoun turned. "The rest of y'all can go," he announced. "Or stay, if you're of a mind to."

The three townspeople wasted no time in heading for the door. They cast glances of fear and relief at Calhoun as they hurried along.

Calhoun walked toward the one table in the room. On it was a metal box. He looked it over, figuring it contained the money stolen from the travelers. It was locked.

"Where's the key, Miss Erline?" he asked.

"Rollie had it on him all the time. Hangin' 'round his neck by a thong."

Calhoun strode outside. The town was still deserted, but he suspected that the residents were watching surreptitiously. He knelt alongside Pepperdine's body, grabbed the rawhide thong, and slit it off.

Inside, he opened the box. It was filled with paper money as well as gold and silver coins. He had never seen so much money all at once before. He almost smiled, thinking how easy it would be to just ride off with it.

He sighed, shut the box, and locked it. He had done some illegal things in his life, but never against people like the emigrants, who could ill afford to lose this money.

He dragged the table and three chairs toward the back wall. He sat, satisfied that he could command the whole room at a glance. Then he walked over and knelt by Erline Rae and Clair. "Food's about ready," he said. He averted his eyes from Clair's bare flesh.

"I'm not hungry," Clair said weakly.

"You got to eat," Erline Rae said. She had been through as much as Clair, but she was inured to such hardships. She was also more practical.

Calhoun and Erline Rae helped Clair up and walked her to the table and sat her down. "Pull yourself together," Erline Rae said to Clair.

Almost absentmindedly, Clair tugged the ends of her dress together and hooked the two remaining buttons. The townswoman began setting out plates and utensils.

Calhoun reloaded his Dragoon, finishing just as the townswoman placed a Dutch oven of stew and a platter of biscuits on the table. A big pot of coffee followed a moment later.

"Thank you, ma'am," Calhoun said quietly. "You can join us, or leave."

"I'd rather leave," the woman squawked.

Calhoun nodded, already ladling stew onto his plate. He dug in as the woman walked away. Calhoun did justice to the stew, which was, he thought, excellent. Erline Rae ate well, too, but Clair hardly touched her food.

When she was done, Erline Rae asked, "What do we do now, Wade?"

Calhoun noticed that the front door was open a little and that several people were peering in. He ignored them mostly, except to keep some of his senses turned in that direction just in case.

"Stay the night here, I reckon, if the people won't mind. Head out in the morning. We push it, we should be able to cut the trail in a week or so."

"What's gonna happen to us?" Erline Rae asked. "Me and Clair, I mean."

Calhoun shrugged. "Life's what you make of it."

Erline Rae smiled. She was sure she would make it. With all the practice she had had at deception, she was certain she could convince some man in Oregon that she was a fine catch.

Besides, she figured, there was always Lee Wilkins. He was only a year or so younger than Erline Rae. He was hard-working, strong, and somewhat handsome. He didn't have the experience of a man like Wade Calhoun, but he made up for that lack with a hound dog–like devotion to her.

Erline Rae was not all that displeased with her

possibilities. She might have preferred spending her time with Calhoun, but she had long ago written that off as hopeless. He had been nothing more than an interlude. An exciting, lusty, passionate diversion, yes, but still, only temporary.

"What about me?" Clair asked. Though her voice was a mere whisper, it came out as something of a wail.

"What about you?" Calhoun asked mildly.

"I don't want to go back to that wagon train," Clair blubbered. "I can't face them, what with them knowin' what Rollie and those others . . . what they did . . . what I went through . . . what . . ." She began crying again.

"Why not?" Erline Rae asked.

"I ain't like you, Erline," she said around her sniffles. "I ain't . . . I mean I . . . you . . ." She paused.

"You mean you ain't been abused before this?" Erline Rae asked harshly. "You mean you ain't had more than one man? You weren't despoiled at a tender young age like I was? That what you mean?"

Erline Rae was angry. She had tried to be nice to Clair all along, trying to help her through the horrors the young widow had undergone. Now she was being paid back with insults.

"I . . . I didn't mean—"

"Like blazes you didn't," Erline Rae snapped. "You . . ."

"Enough," Calhoun said quietly but with force. He sighed, as he rolled a cigarette. "You know damn well she ain't had your kind of life, Erline," Calhoun said after the cigarette was going. "She ain't used to such doin's. You know how to cope with these things. She don't."

"But, Wade . . ."

"Quiet." Calhoun wasn't angry, but he wanted no argument.

Erline Rae was irate, but she clamped her mouth shut.

"You ain't lived much of a respectable life," Calhoun continued. "That it wasn't your doin' don't matter. You learned to deal with it. You know damn well you can go to Oregon and pretend like none of it happened; that you can talk some feller into believin' you're pure as the snow." He half grinned.

Erline Rae began to soften a little, knowing that what he said was true.

"Clair ain't had no experience at such things. She was young, married her first beau, then lost him in an Indian attack. She was stole away and violated. Hard to take for someone's led a sheltered life, don't you think?"

"Yes," Erline Rae admitted. She felt sick that she could ever think poorly of Clair Wright. The young woman might be a weepy thing, but she had stood up under the worst that Pepperdine and the others could dish out. She had cried about it, seemingly constantly, but she had not broken.

"Then what're we gonna do about it?" Erline Rae asked.

Calhoun came as close to a smile as he ever did. "We help her lie."

"What?" Clair asked, head coming up and tears stopping as if dammed.

"We'll just tell all those folks you wasn't abused."

"They won't believe that," Clair whispered, shame overtaking her again.

"Sure they will." He paused. "If you make them believe that."

"How?" Clair asked. She tried not to let the hope that had blossomed take hold of her, lest she be too disappointed.

"We tell 'em Pepperdine and the others knew I was hard on their trail, and that they was afraid of me. They'll believe that, after . . ." He paused. He saw no need to rehash his run-ins with Pepperdine, North, and some of the others. "You tell 'em Pepperdine was afraid to take the time to defile you.

"But it's been so long since we left. The folks with the wagon train won't buy that I was three weeks or so with them and untouched." It was getting more difficult to battle the hope.

"So, tell 'em it was only five, six days maybe; that you was taken straight south. It took us the rest of the time to mosey on back up there."

Clair's eyes were bright. "You think it'll work?" she asked, heart pounding. The possibility of starting anew was exciting. It was tempered by fear, disgust, and loss. She did not think she would ever get over what had happened to her, but she thought maybe if she could keep it suppressed she might find a good new life. Maybe even find another husband.

Doing that might even be easier when she bore her child. It would prove to a beau that she was fertile. Being a young widow, with her husband having been killed by Indians would be no hindrance. She was certain she would never find another man as good as Mike Wright, but still, there were a lot of men and few women in Oregon. She should have a choice.

"It'll work," Calhoun said. "Those folks might think differently, but I doubt any'll say anything. Doin' so would be callin' you a liar. It'll also be callin' me a liar, and they won't want to do that. Even after I leave."

It was almost two more weeks before they caught the wagon train, somewhere out in the westernmost stretch of the Snake River Plain.

Calhoun and Erline Rae had coached Clair on her new role along the trail. After some initial trepidation and worry, Clair showed signs of progress. By the time they spotted the wagon train, she was comfortable with what she had to do.

She had even gotten used to the sight and sound of Calhoun and Erline Rae coupling every night. It had bothered her at first, bringing back the sour memories of Pepperdine's men. It also brought back memories of her husband, though. She was ashamed to learn that she yearned for a man's intimate touch. It took her a few nights—and some sincere conversation with Erline Rae—to realize such yearnings were not shameful or unnatural.

As he sat on a ridge watching the wagons plod along, pulling into the night's camp formation, Calhoun considered sending the two women down alone with the box of money. But he had been hired on to do a job—take this wagon train to Oregon—and he would not shirk that duty.

He waited until the camp was mostly set up, then he, Erline Rae, and Clair rode down. It was not yet dark, for which he was grateful. He would hate to have come all this way only to get shot by a nervous emigrant.

They were welcomed with excitement and wonder. Polly greeted Calhoun diffidently. She knew he would be gone soon, and wanted to prepare herself for that. Calhoun accepted it, thankful that he would not have to hurt her when he rode off.

After Barrett Coldhammer introduced the three to the new guide he had hired back at Fort Hall, everyone gathered around Coldhammer's campfire to hear the story told.

Calhoun let the women do most of the talking. Erline Rae, as was expected, had no trouble. He was proud to hear Clair tell her falsehoods without flinching.

Afterward, the people drifted off. Clair was taken under the protection of Gus Stewart's family and whisked away. Erline Rae headed for her wagon, after whispering to Calhoun that she expected to see him soon. She smiled at Lee Wilkins and told him she would see him in the morning. The young man was disappointed, but he said nothing as he left.

Finally only Calhoun, Coldhammer, and the new guide, Wes Morehouse, were sitting at the fire. "I'd be obliged was you to see how the camp is, Wes," Coldhammer said.

Morehouse looked at him in question. Then he nodded, knowing Coldhammer wanted time to talk with Calhoun alone. He left.

Coldhammer pulled out a bottle of whiskey and passed it to Calhoun. A cigar followed moments later.

"I didn't know if you was comin' back, Mister Calhoun," Coldhammer said. There was no apology in his voice. "When I had the chance to hire Mister Morehouse at Fort Hall, I did so."

Calhoun nodded. "It was wise. That's a rough stretch west of the fort."

They were silent for a moment. Then Calhoun said quietly, "I'll expect the rest of my pay, considerin'."

Coldhammer nodded. He thought it only right. He still had the box sitting next to him. He opened it, counted out one hundred dollars in coin, and handed the money to Calhoun.

"You're welcome to ride along, if you like," Coldhammer said. He coughed a little in embarrassment. "Maybe to accompany Miss Erline . . ." He left it dangling.

"I'm obliged," he said noncommittally. A few minutes later, he was climbing into Erline Rae's wagon. She was waiting for him with open arms, and a willing hungriness that said she knew he would be leaving soon.

Calhoun left the camp in the dark. It was still an hour or so before dawn. Erline Rae had come only half awake when he rose. He had kissed her once, lightly, before easing his way out of the wagon. He stopped now, just outside the camp, looking back at the twinkling of the fires.

Then he turned his horse's head southward. He had been to California before, and had always found it an agreeable place. With a pack mule in tow, he rode off.

the punishment of traitors . . . .

Then he turned to his companions, and, as if
talking of ordinary concerns, bade them seek
the pleasant places where a just man might find
repose.

CLINT HAWKINS is the pseudonym of a newspaper editor and writer who lives in Phoenix, Arizona.

VALLEY OF WILD HORSES
0-06-100221-6 $3.95

WILDERNESS TREK
0-06-100260-7 $3.99

THE VANISHING AMERICAN
0-06-100295-X $3.99

CAPTIVES OF THE DESERT
0-06-100292-5 $3.99

THE SPIRIT OF THE BORDER
0-06-100293-3 $3.99

BLACK MESA
0-06-100291-7 $3.99

ROBBERS' ROOST
0-06-100280-1 $3.99

UNDER THE TONTO RIM
0-06-100294-1 $3.99

**For Fastest Service–
Visa & MasterCard
Holders Call
1-800-331-3761**

MAIL TO: Harper Collins Publishers
P. O. Box 588 Dunmore, PA 18512-0588
OR CALL: (800) 331-3761 (Visa/MasterCard)

Yes, please send me the books I have checked:

❑ THE DUDE RANGER (0-06-100055-8)	$3.50	❑ THE CODE OF THE WEST (0-06-100173-2)	$3.50
❑ THE LOST WAGON TRAIN (0-06-100064-7)	$3.99	❑ ARIZONA AMES (0-06-100171-6)	$3.50
❑ WILDFIRE (0-06-100081-7)	$3.50	❑ ROGUE RIVER FEUD (0-06-100214-3)	$3.95
❑ THE MAN OF THE FOREST (0-06-100082-5)	$3.95	❑ THE THUNDERING HERD (0-06-100217-8)	$3.95
❑ THE BORDER LEGION (0-06-100083-3)	$3.95	❑ HORSE HEAVEN HILL (0-06-100210-0)	$3.95
❑ SUNSET PASS (0-06-100084-1)	$3.50	❑ VALLEY OF WILD HORSES (0-06-100221-6)	$3.95
❑ 30,000 ON HOOF (0-06-100085-X)	$3.50	❑ WILDERNESS TREK (0-06-100260-7)	$3.99
❑ THE WANDERER OF THE WASTELAND		❑ THE VANISHING AMERICAN (0-06-100295-X)	$3.99
(0-06-100092-2)	$3.50	❑ CAPTIVES OF THE DESERT (0-06-100292-5)	$3.99
❑ TWIN SOMBREROS (0-06-100101-5)	$3.50	❑ THE SPIRIT OF THE BORDER (0-06-100293-3)	$3.99
❑ BOULDER DAM (0-06-100111-2)	$3.50	❑ BLACK MESA (0-06-100291-7)	$3.99
❑ THE TRAIL DRIVER (0-06-100154-6)	$3.50	❑ ROBBERS' ROOST (0-06-100280-1)	$3.99
❑ TO THE LAST MAN (0-06-100218-6)	$3.50	❑ UNDER THE TONTO RIM (0-06-100294-1)	$3.99
❑ THUNDER MOUNTAIN (0-06-100216-X)	$3.50		

SUBTOTAL ....$_____

POSTAGE AND HANDLING ....$ 2.00*

SALES TAX (Add applicable sales tax) ....$_____

TOTAL: $_____

*ORDER 4 OR MORE TITLES AND POSTAGE & HANDLING IS FREE!
Orders of less than 4 books, please include $2.00 p/h. Remit in US funds, do not send cash.

Name _____

Address _____

City _____ State _____ Zip _____

(Valid only in US & Canada) Allow up to 6 weeks delivery. Prices subject to change.   HO301

Saddle-up to these

THE REGULATOR *by Dale Colter*
Sam Slater, blood brother of the Apache and a cunning bounty-hunter, is out to collect the big price on the heads of the murderous Pauley gang. He'll give them a single choice: surrender and live, or go for your sixgun.

THE REGULATOR—Diablo At Daybreak *by Dale Colter*
The Governor wants the blood of the Apache murderers who ravaged his daughter. He gives Sam Slater a choice: work for him, or face a noose. Now Slater must hunt down the deadly renegade Chacon…Slater's Apache brother.

THE JUDGE *by Hank Edwards*
Federal Judge Clay Torn is more than a judge—sometimes he has to be the jury *and* the executioner. Torn pits himself against the most violent and ruthless man in Kansas, a battle whose final verdict will judge one man right…and one man dead.

THE JUDGE—War Clouds *by Hank Edwards*
Judge Clay Torn rides into Dakota where the Cheyenne are painting for war and the army is shining steel and loading lead. If war breaks out, someone is going to make a pile of money on a river of blood.